W9-AYW-672

TEMPEST IN A TEA ROOM

TEA TIME COZY MYSTERIES, BOOK 1

SUMMER PRESCOTT

SUMMER PRESCOTT BOOKS PUBLISHING

CHAPTER ONE

Delaney Powers' phone rang early Saturday morning, the vibrations on the nightstand next to her rudely interrupting a much-needed sleep. With a frustrated groan, she flipped onto her stomach and pulled the pillow over her head to muffle the obnoxious sound, but ultimately she couldn't bring herself to ignore the incoming call.

"Who on earth is calling at 7 a.m. on a Saturday?" she grumbled, glancing at her ancient clock radio.

Her brow furrowed in a sleepy frown, Delaney sat up and swiped a finger across the screen of her smartphone to accept the call, not even bothering to check the number. If the caller happened to be a poor, unsuspecting telemarketer, she would try her best to contain her wrath and summon an appropriate response.

"Hello?" Her voice was less than warm.

"Laney, it's me."

The sound of her boyfriend's voice helped bring her to life…a bit.

"Ben? Hey, sweetie. It's a little early, isn't it?"

There was a hesitation on the other end of the line, and Delaney could just picture Ben pulling out his grandfather's pocket watch and realizing the time.

"Oh…yeah, sorry. I've been up for a while. I just assumed it was later. Do you want me to, uhh…?" He sounded adorably flustered.

"It's ok. I'll forgive you…this time." Laney smiled, rubbed her eyes with her free hand, and flung her messy braid over her shoulder. "What's going on?"

She rose languidly and stretched, anticipating a sneak preview of one of the stories that was about to hit the presses. Having a boyfriend who was an editor at one of the world's leading newspapers meant that she always heard the exciting news first, but typically those kinds of calls came late in the evening once the stories had been posted and sent to print.

"Well, the thing is, I'm here…outside your building, I mean," he admitted. "Can you come down? I really need to talk to you."

Delaney cut her stretch short, slowly lowering her hands, and her stomach did a queasy little flip-flop. She knew from the tone of his voice that Ben wasn't going to be delivering the latest scoop on the celebrities spotted at the city's top restaurants and wondered what might have happened to make him sound so odd.

"Of course," she replied immediately, doing her level best to tamp down the tickle of concern that rose up within her. "I'll be right down."

Laney grabbed her wire-rimmed glasses from the dresser, glad that she'd worn yoga pants and a t-shirt to bed, slid into a pair of sandals, and made sure her keys were in her pocket before locking the door and scurrying down the two flights of stairs to W 69th Street. She spotted Ben sitting on a bench next to the entrance of Central Park.

Wanting to put a smile on his face, after hearing his strange manner on the phone, Laney approached Ben from behind and placed her arms around his neck, planting a kiss on his cheek. She was more than a touch surprised when his body stiffened.

"We need to talk." He nodded at the vacant bench beside him, avoiding her gaze. Puzzled, Delaney moved to the other side of the bench. In the two years that they'd been together, Ben had never behaved this way. It made her wonder if he'd been fired, or something equally horrible.

"Alright." She sank down onto the bench, tucking one leg beneath her, her stomach fluttering. When she looked over at Ben, Laney saw the slightly crumpled letters in his lap and her adrenaline went through the roof.

"Where did you get those?" she asked quietly.

"Does it matter, Delaney?" He sighed and shook his head, his eyes pained. "Why didn't you tell me about all these?" He held up the stack of five or six job offer letters she had received over the past year.

Busted. She couldn't avoid talking about the rather uncomfortable subject any longer, and truthfully, she resented Ben a bit for forcing the issue. They'd been living their lives and coexisting peacefully...until now. Laney opened her mouth to explain, twisting her fingers together in her lap, but before she could utter a word, Ben cut her off.

"You told me we couldn't move in together because you're still freelancing - that you didn't have a steady income." He swallowed hard and looked away, his tone colored with accusation.

She nodded, staring at the concrete sidewalk in front of the bench. "Yeah, I know."

"But all this time you had the chance to land a regular job." He held out the papers like a fan of playing cards. "Every one of these companies wanted to take you on as an illustrator."

Delancy's defenses slammed into place like steel walls. She would've hoped that he'd understand, but it seemed that his relational needs had overcome his capacity for empathy.

"I told you when we started dating that I'm an artist, Ben. I have no interest in selling out like..." Laney could feel the heat rise in her cheeks as she clamped her mouth shut.

"Like who? Me?" he asked quietly.

Delaney stared down the street, at a tragic-looking mime who couldn't seem to get out of an imaginary window. She swallowed past a lump in her throat and shook her head. She had no words to offer at the moment.

"I took the job at the newspaper so that I could do what I love and still pay my bills. Just because I'm not a starving artist anymore, doesn't mean I'm not a real writer," Ben said dully.

Delaney wondered absently whether he was trying to convince her or himself.

"I'm not you," she whispered, her eyes welling with tears.

Ben tossed the wad of letters into the trash can beside the bench and stood. Laney craned her neck and tilted her head up to meet his gaze. Every trace of warmth and compassion had fled from his chocolate eyes and his next words sounded so mechanical that they might as well have come from the disc-shaped robot who vacuumed her apartment.

"I can't do this anymore - I'm done."

Part of Delaney wanted to beg him not to go - to promise that she'd change - but in the end, she merely stared up at him from her spot on the cold, unyielding bench. She refused to apologize for who she was. Deep down she knew that if Ben couldn't accept something so fundamental about her, clearly they weren't meant to be together. To sacrifice her way of life, her passion, for him, would only do them both harm and would be a roller coaster ride to failure. It was like dealing with her parents all over again. All she'd ever wanted from them was acceptance, and they couldn't offer even that. Apparently, neither could Ben.

When he turned to walk down the street and back to his office, Delaney didn't stop him. She stared after him, until he disappeared around the corner, then dropped her gaze to take in the iridescent cast on the feathers of a strutting pigeon at her feet. Eventually, she rose and strolled wistfully home, stopping to check the mail before she hiked back up to her studio. Once inside, Delaney sank down into her burnt-orange thrift store love seat, feeling as though she had just run a marathon...or had been hit by a truck. The same truck that seemed to circle her from time to time when it came to making life decisions.

She sifted rather mindlessly through the mail – it was easier to busy herself with mundane tasks, rather than facing the emotional upheaval that Ben had just wrought - and tossed the junk mail aside. She stopped short, her heart rate accelerating a bit, when she discovered an envelope with a stamp that said TIME SENSITIVE. The return address was in Iberden, VT - her Grandma Marcy's hometown. Grandma Marcy was the only relative who still spoke to Laney after her parents kicked her out...but the dear woman had died back in April.

Carefully tearing open the linen-like envelope as though it might hold a secrct from the grave, she unfolded the letter, on official letterhead, and read the first few lines. It was from a law office in Iberden, and legalese aside, it seemed as though Grandma Marcy had left her something.

The two of them had been close, but when Grandma Marcy had passed away a few months ago, there had never been any revelation of a will. Laney had been so overcome with grief at the time, that she hadn't even thought about who might inherit her grandmother's earthly possessions. She pored over the legal jargon until she reached a passage highlighted in bold.

8

Marcy's Tea Room

23 Maple Path

Iberden, VT 05402

Marcy's Tea Room had been one of the most popular places in the quaint little town of Iberden, particularly for tourists, but ten years ago, Grandma Marcy had inexplicably closed the booming business. Delaney remembered her grandmother insisting that the tea room stay in the family, but the thought that she would be the one to inherit it had never crossed her mind.

She called the number on the letter, as instructed, and reached the office of Janet O'Shea. The woman who answered was quick to offer her sympathies when Delaney introduced herself, she

"Oh, honey," Janet said softly, "I'm so sorry for your loss."

Tears tracked slowly down Laney's cheeks as she tried valiantly to maintain her composure, chewing on her bottom lip while listening numbly to the details of her grandma's will.

"But did she say why she left it to me?" Delaney asked when the process for the transfer of assets had been explained.

"She left you a note," Janet replied, sounding a bit evasive. "But I was instructed to give it to you in person - here, in Iberden."

Without pausing for thought or missing a beat, Delaney replied, "I'll be there tonight."

Was she using the situation as an excuse to flee from dealing with her memories of Ben and the pain that their breakup had caused? Probably. But what better reason than to attend to the affairs of her beloved grandmother?

CHAPTER TWO

The bus doors opened with a hydraulic wheeze at the last stop on the route. Delaney, the only passenger remaining, stepped down and waited for the driver to retrieve her luggage. After the nine-hour ride from NYC, she was more than relieved to finally be able to stretch her legs.

A glorious sunset that painted the sky in brilliant shades of pink and orange, nearly took her breath away, and Delaney stood transfixed, memories of visits with Grandma Marcy warming her heart. She was reluctantly pulled back to the present by the rumbling sound of the bus pulling away. Her purple suitcase had been politely set on the curb beside her.

Delaney glanced at her phone and was relieved to see she still had a little time to spare before her meeting with Janet O'Shea at the Tea Room. Tucking the phone into her back pocket, she glanced up at the map of Iberden, prominently displayed behind plexiglass at the bus stop.

Maple Path was the main road through the center of town. It was dotted with businesses and homes that were charming, tidy, and well-kept. The winding lanes extending out to the newer residential areas were few and far between in the small town. As luck would have it, Laney discovered that the bus had stopped on the far end of the main road and she began to meander toward town, mindful of her target destination and hoping to get her bearings.

The road wasn't fully paved – it graduated to gravel at the sides - and there were no sidewalks, at least this far out. According to the map, once she got closer to the town proper, she'd see more signs of civilization. After dragging and scraping her suitcase over the gravel-strewn road for about a mile, she passed a small sandwich shop on her right, next door to the post office and on the left she saw a new yarn shop and a coffee roastery. The thought of fresh coffee made her mouth water, but Delaney didn't stop until she stood gazing up at the familiar, weathered sign for Marcy's Tea Room.

There were soft lights glowing behind the front windows, and despite the waning daylight outside, Delaney could make out two figures sitting at a large table toward the back of the shop. Her phone vibrated in her pocket, and she pulled it out, not surprised at all to see Janet O'Shea's number lighting up her screen. She hit the answer button.

"Hi, Janet, I'm actually just now walking up the porch steps."

Delaney still had the phone to her ear as she knocked on the heavy wooden door.

"Wonderful," Janet replied. "We'll be right there."

We?

Delaney wasn't expecting to meet anyone else, so she was surprised when a tall and lanky woman with short curly hair, who looked to be about her own age, opened the door to reveal a paunchy, elderly man with wisps of gray hair tucked beneath a black baseball cap, standing next to her. Both Janet and the man smiled.

"Please come in, come in." Janet led the way into the tea room.

Oddly, rather than introducing himself, the elderly man merely stepped aside to allow Laney to follow Janet. As the trio moved into the dining area, Delaney noticed that all the tables had a thick layer of dust covering them, as if to drive the point home that the once-busy tea room had been out of service for many years, though Grandma Marcy had still used the massive Victorian home as her primary residence. The white damask tablecloths, the hand-tatted lace curtains, and the cobwebbed, ornate chandelier hanging from the cciling hearkened back to the tea room's glory days, when only the best trappings would do. Grandma Marcy had a keen eye for detail and chose only the finest materials for her tea room.

The glow that Laney had seen from the front of the building came from three white taper candles flickering in a tarnished candelabra that sat in the middle of a round table in the very back of the dining arca. Thankfully, this table had apparently been dusted and looked as though it might have been in use recently. The thought that crossed her mind as the threc of them took their seats was that if one of those candles happened to fall out of the candelabra, the tea room would be toast…quite literally. It seemed more than a bit odd that she was meeting with the attorney by candlelight, with a total stranger present, but, figuring that she'd be brought up to speed shortly, Laney kept her mouth shut, settled into a rickety wooden chair with one leg shorter than the other three, and folded her hands in her lap.

Janet withdrew a folder from the oversized purse that was hanging on the back of her chair and slid it over to Delaney. The man finally reached out his hand and introduced himself with a smile.

"Hi, Laney, I'm Roger. It's nice to be able to put a face with your name. Your grandma spoke very highly of you."

He looked at her expectantly and Delaney smiled politely, frantically searching her whirling brain for a proper response. Roger seemed to register the confusion in her eyes, and his smile dimmed. "You don't know who I am, do you?"

Delaney shook her head and shrugged apologetically. "I'm sorry. Were you one of Grandma Marcy's friends?"

Janet shifted uncomfortably in her chair, looking like she wanted to be anywhere but there, and looked to Roger for a response.

"Well, in a way, yes." Roger's reply was quiet, and his hands, as he looked down at them, shook a bit. "Marcy and I were going to get married this year, but, as I'm sure you know, the cancer was more aggressive than anyone had expected..." He trailed off, leaving the final words unspoken.

"I'm so sorry." Delaney managed to hold back a gasp. Grandma Marcy had made no mention of a fiancé... which she found odd.

Her heart went out to the grieving old man in front of her. She knew firsthand how painful it was to lose a loved one...she'd lost more than her share of them through the years. They hadn't died – that might have even been less painful – no, they'd simply shut her out. She still felt a profound sense of loss. Before Roger could regain his composure and reply, there was a soft knock on the front door.

Janet tilted her head to look out the front window, then cupped her hands around her mouth and called out, "Come in Mayor Andrews. We're just getting started."

The door burst open and a broad man in a finely-tailored navy blue suit strode to the table. He was so tall that he nearly had to duck down to enter the dining area in the rear of the old Victorian, where the ceilings were lower. His sleek, black hair was plastered to his head with what had to be a copious amount of hair product, and each step he took made the shop's ancient floorboards rattle and squeak beneath him.

Flashing a smile at Laney, Mayor Andrews remained standing when he reached the table in a few quick strides, towering over the others.

"You must be Delaney. We're so glad to have you here in Iberden, though of course, the current circumstances aren't exactly ideal." The mayor affected a meekly mournful expression that was so in conflict with his larger-than-life personality that it was almost comical. Almost.

His ersatz sympathy didn't fool Laney for a minute. Something about him made the hair on her nape stand up in warning, but she accepted his condolences graciously.

"Well." Janet cleared her throat, clearly ready to get down to business. "Now that we're all here, let's get started."

She opened the folder facing Delaney. "This is Marcy Dellin's will, which states that you, Miss Delaney Powers, are the sole beneficiary of Marcy's Tea Room."

She removed a small, sealed envelope from one of the pockets of the folder and handed it to Laney. "And this, is a personal note from your grandmother. I was instructed to give it to you to be opened immediately after you were informed of her final wishes regarding the Tea Room. It is to be read only by you, and the contents of it should not be shared after the fact. Those were her exact instructions," Janet explained solemnly.

Delaney silently opened the envelop and read the poignant words on the scrap of paper.

Sometimes the roughest of things can be made smooth again with just a little love from the right person. Love my tea room as I have loved it, dear Laney. Love it as only you can.

The familiar penmanship brought tears to her eyes, and Delaney could swear that she heard her grandma's voice as she read the words. Though she didn't understand why the note had to be kept a secret, Delaney knew that Grandma Marcy wouldn't have given those instructions unless they were important. Without a word to anyone present, just like Grandma Marcy had asked, she folded the note and tucked it into the pocket of her jeans. When she looked up, lost in memories, and blinking back tears, the others were still staring at her.

"Erm...anything else?" she asked, gazing at Janet, overwhelmed, and trying to take it all in.

Janet and Roger both looked rather uncomfortable, as though they wanted to speak, but didn't quite know what to say. Mayor Andrews, on the other hand, had a frown on his face that bordered on a glare. The friendly facade slipped momentarily, and he grimaced, swallowing hard. Then, seeming to snap back into character, he shook his head and slid the fake smile firmly back into place.

"I'm sorry," he addressed Delaney, his tone so saccharin that she instinctively recoiled. "I know that this must be a very difficult time for you, and maybe it's not the best time to mention it but, I feel like you should know that Marcy and I were negotiating a business deal before she died."

Janet's mouth was set in a firm line, her expression seeming deliberately neutral, and Roger's hands curled into fists at his sides, making Laney wonder what she was missing.

"You see," Mayor Andrews continued, clearly oblivious to the reactions that his words had inspired. "I had made an offer to buy Marcy's Tea Room, at the beginning of the year, but unfortunately, we didn't get to finalize the paperwork before your dear grandmother passed."

Delaney stared at the mayor in disbelief, a white-hot fury flashing through her veins. She fought to maintain control of her temper when she spoke.

"You're here – while I'm still mourning my grandmother - because you missed your chance to buy the tea room and thought you could convince me, in the midst of my grief, to sell it to you?"

Laney's eyes flashed fire as she stood to face the mayor. She squared her shoulders and rose up to her full 5'3" height.

"I didn't just fall off of the hay truck and I wasn't born yesterday. I will not be taken advantage of no matter how clouded my thinking might be at the moment. It was in incredibly poor taste for you to come here this evening, Mayor Andrews. I'm here tonight to hear my grandmother's wishes and read her final words to me, none of which has anything to do with you."

Folding her arms over her chest, Laney glanced pointedly at the door, then back at the mayor.

A dark fury momentarily colored his features. It was so fleeting that Laney wondered if she imagined it, because in an instant, the oily smile was back

"Of course. How clumsy of me. Take all the time you need, and I'll be in touch."

There was a knife-sharp edge to his parting glance before he turned on his heel and headed for the door, leaving Laney trembling where she stood.

Janet stood up next. "I think I'll be going too, unless you have any questions."

Miserable, Laney wrapped her arms around her midsection and shook her head, her heart pounding after her encounter with the mayor. Roger stuffed his hands in his pockets, a hangdog look on his face, and realization hit Delaney like a lightning bolt. The house above and around the tea room hadn't just been her Grandma's home; it must've been Roger's too. Her heart ached for the sad old man who looked as lost as Laney felt.

"Roger, why don't you show me around? I'm sure there has to be a guest room in the living area upstairs, right?" she asked.

"Really?" His eyes went wide. "You…you'll let me stay?" His voice was hoarse and filled with hope.

"I insist," Laney said softly. If Roger had been important to Grandma Marcy, he was important to her as well.

She turned to Janet, who had closed the file folder on the table and picked up her purse, ready to head for the door. "I think we're all good here for now. I'm sure Roger will get me up to speed on what I need to know about the tea room in the morning."

"I've left your copy of the will in the folder." Janet inclined her head toward the table. "Let me know if you have any questions after I leave. Your grandma was a dear person, and I know she loved you very much," she said softly, squeezing Laney's shoulder before she left, closing the door gently behind her.

"It's been a long trip." Laney suddenly felt all done in and Roger took the hint that she was calling it a night.

"The guest bedroom is all set up. Sweet Marcy was always ready to host company, even though visitors were rare. Up the stairs and to the right," Roger directed. "Goodnight, Laney."

Delaney was sweetly surprised that he had used her nickname, but then…why wouldn't he? Grandma Marcy was the one who had given her the nickname all those years ago. Overcome by nostalgia, she smiled at the stranger who had been her grandma's beloved, because deep down, it felt good to be Laney again.

"Goodnight."

CHAPTER THREE

The next day, without much internal conflict at all, Laney made a bold decision and sprang into action. No one seemed to know why Marcy had closed her aging, yet still very popular tea room. In fact, closing the booming business had actually seemed to stir up quite a bit of angst amongst the townspeople. While some argued that the rundown space could be renovated and put to better use, others claimed that closing the pillar of the Iberden downtown would confuse tourists who had returned to the cozy spot year after year.

Laney's mind whirled with possibilities. She planned to restore Marcy's Tea Room and open it to the public once again, as soon as possible. The opportunity couldn't have come at a more perfect time. Her lease in New York was ending this month, Ben had taken himself out of the picture, and she could freelance from anywhere. Really, there was nothing to lose by making her grandmother's last wishes a reality.

While Grandma Marcy had probably intended that Laney treat the tea room simply as a home, just the way that Marcy had when she closed the business, Laney couldn't think of a better way to honor her grandma than to bring back the establishment that had given her such joy. She would treat it like a freelance art project and was giddy with excitement at the prospect of taking something old and a bit too formal and transforming it into a warm and inviting space where all felt welcome.

With a wonderfully heady sense of freedom and purpose, the city girl strolled down Maple Path. After stopping for a latte that would rival any that she'd had in the city, along with a decadent croissant, at the coffee roastery, Delaney made a beeline for Babby's Antiques, determined to spend the majority of her day using her meager savings to purchase items that would bring Marcy's Tea Room back to life. Since her home had been in the heart of NYC for the past few years, Laney found the abundance of small-town charm to be both a breath of fresh air and a bit of a culture shock. She felt as though she'd suddenly been transported onto the set of a Hallmark movie, which was utterly charming and a touch surreal.

Entering the shop which smelled like the lovely combination of potpourri and wood oil, Laney was immediately drawn to a mismatched collection of Persian rugs. Transfixed by the quality and color assortment that she found as she turned back the corners of the beautiful rugs, she jumped, startled, when she felt a sudden tap on her shoulder. Turning quickly, with a gasp, she encountered the bird-like little elderly woman who had been behind the counter just a minute ago, standing less than a foot from her.

"Finding everything, dear?"

The woman peered at Laney from behind round, wire-framed spectacles, much like her own, and smiled, her eyes crinkling at the corners.

Laney let out a breath and laughed at herself for her reaction. Strangers generally didn't just randomly tap on you in New York, so she'd been entirely unprepared for the simple touch.

"Oh, yes, thank you. This place is so wonderfully eclectic – I know I'll be able to find some items here that will be just perfect for my project."

"Well, isn't that nice. I'm Babby, and from the talk of the town, you must be Laney."

She patted Laney's shoulder with a frail-looking hand. "I'll be over behind the counter, but don't hesitate to call me if you need any help. We've got a fine collection in here - you won't find these kinds of items anywhere within a hundred miles," she assured Laney, beaming with pride.

"Thank you so much." Laney returned Babby's grin and went back to examining the rugs.

After taking a close look at four rugs that were rolled up and leaning against the wall, she planned to purchase three of them for the tea room - one for the entrance, one for the hallway, and one for the parlor. Laney meandered through aisles of treasures from days gone by to the back of the store where china and silverware displays caught her attention.

There were at least ten gorgeous tea sets on display, in all different colors and patterns. One, in particular, she absolutely loved. It was primarily pink, with cabbage roses and bright green leaves winding around the cups and plates like a happy floral hug. Calculating the number of tables that she wanted to keep in the main room, Laney decided that seven tea sets would do, for now. She was planning ahead – ideally, if the tea room got particularly busy, there would still be plenty of clean dishes and plates for guests.

Many of the tables that were still in the tea room didn't have chairs with them, so next she selected an assortment of chairs for each table, all of them wooden so that she'd be able to paint them to coordinate with each other, despite their different styles. She could also re-upholster them in matching fabrics to achieve a more cohesive look.

Mentally tallying the costs in her head as she made her way to the cash register, Laney realized, much to her chagrin, that she had no way to transport her purchases back to the tea room.

"Find a few things, honey?" Babby asked, looking up from her crossword puzzle and sliding carefully off the tall stool behind the register.

"Quite a few things, actually." Laney nodded. "But I'm afraid I don't know how I'm going to get them to the tea room."

"Oh, don't you worry about that. Matt Nelson – he's our local mailman – does in-town deliveries for a small fee. He can drop it off for you lickety-split," Babby assured her. "He's been working for me on the side for years."

"That's fantastic, thank you so much. Do you know roughly when he'll be delivering?"

"Probably within half an hour." Babby handed her a credit card slip and Laney signed it, letting out a sigh of relief.

She had a ton of cleaning and sprucing up to do, but somehow knowing that the furniture, rugs, china, and silverware would be arriving soon spurred her to action. Thanking Babby one last time, she left the cute little shop and headed back to the tea room, stopping to window shop and admire the natural beauty around her along the way. Lured in once again by the tantalizing aroma of freshly roasted coffee beans, she picked up a decaf latte to-go, and sipped it as she meandered toward the tea room. Relaxed by the charming walk through town, her mind whirling with thoughts of paint colors and furniture arrangement, Laney had just gotten to the front door of her new graceful Victorian home when an unfamiliar voice surprised her from the driveway beside the house.

"Hey, there!"

Laney jumped and dropped her key on the welcome mat, thinking that she really needed to be less fearful in this safe little town. City habits were hard to break, it seemed. She turned and saw a man in uniform leaning against a postal truck parked on the driveway in front of the detached garage beside the house. She'd been so lost in thought that she'd walked right past and hadn't even noticed the truck.

"I'm Matt." The gangly mailman with a wide grin and a mop of strawberry blond hair trotted up the steps to shake her hand. "Babby told me you wanted this stuff dropped off - hope it's ok that I got here a little early."

"It's wonderful that you got here early. Actually, you were probably right on time, I just dawdled on my way home. I can't help myself, this is such a charming town." Laney smiled, delighted. "I hate to impose, but, if you don't mind, I could use a little help getting these rugs inside."

"I don't mind at all." Matt turned and headed to his truck. "Go ahead and open the door and we'll get them inside. I can carry the crates of dishes for you too. They're pretty heavy."

"That would be great. Thank you." Laney unlocked and opened the door, then hurried to the truck, offering to lift one end of a rolled up rug to carry it inside.

"No worries, I've got it," Matt assured her. He picked up the first rug and hefted it up onto his shoulder. "Just point me in the right direction."

Laney led him into the main room and gestured to the far wall. "Right there is fine for now." He leaned the rug against the wall, then brought the others in, leaning them side by side.

"Can you please take that last one to the back room?" Laney asked, pointing toward the doorway to the parlor that served as the secondary dining area, when Matt came in with the final rug.

"Not a problem," Matt replied, heading for the doorway.

He'd only taken a couple of steps into the parlor when he froze in place.

"It has to go in the middle," Laney instructed, from behind his left shoulder.

Matt dropped the rug and sprinted into the room, dropping to his knees. Laney looked up, bracing herself against the doorway and gasped when she caught a glimpse of a figure on the floor, mostly hidden by an ancient, dust-covered sofa.

"Roger?" she whispered, horrified.

Matt's body, as he knelt to feel for a pulse, blocked her from getting a better view. "Call 911," he directed.

Laney's heart raced, and her fingers shook as she dragged her phone out of her purse. "What happened to him? What's wrong with Roger?" she asked tearfully, hovering near the doorway and waiting for the dispatcher to answer her call.

Matt took a deep breath and let it out in a whoosh. "It's not Roger - it's Mayor Andrews," he replied. He stood and stepped aside to reveal the man that Laney had just met last night, now clearly lifeless in the middle of her parlor.

CHAPTER FOUR

After confirming that Mayor Andrews was in fact dead, Officer Bill Bonham immediately called the coroner. "We have to determine whether or not the Mayor died of natural causes or if there was foul play," he told Lancy and Matt, whom he'd ordered to wait in the main room for questioning.

"But, I have no idea what he was even doing here," Lancy protested. "It had to be foul play. He wasn't an invited guest, and he certainly didn't have a key…that I know of. I have no idea why he came here, or why he…died." She swallowed hard, trembling at the thought that there was a dead man lying in the next room.

"We'll be doing a thorough investigation, including looking for signs of forced entry, a struggle, and the like, but for now, you two just need to sit tight until I can get a statement from you. I'm sorry Matt, I know you have your route to deliver, but the mail is just going to have to be late today."

Thankfully, Roger had been at the local market all morning, so he was safe from whatever had transpired, but when he saw the police car and ambulance outside the tea room, he barged past the officer standing at the door and rushed into the room.

Laney saw Roger's expression turn from abject fear to concern as he processed the reality that, while she was safe, something was indeed wrong.

"Roger," Officer Bonham held up a hand, addressing him with compassion. "You're going to have to wait outside - at least until the detective and the forensics team get here."

Confused, the elderly man nodded wearily. Shooting a quick look toward Laney, he backed away and closed the door behind him.

Bonham took their initial statements, but instructed them to wait for the homicide detective, in case she had further questions. Laney hoped that the detective would find evidence that explained just exactly what had happened to the mayor in her parlor.

After what seemed an eternity, the front door swung open, drawing everyone's attention to a woman in a black pant suit who had a badge pinned to her chest.

"Detective Worth," Officer Bonham greeted her with a nod. "I didn't expect to see you so soon."

"Are you kidding?" The detective cocked an eyebrow at him. "A potential homicide case in Iberden is big news. This is the first we've heard from your department since that cold case from the 90s. The chief sent me as soon as he hung up with you."

Detective Worth directed her sharp-eyed gaze toward Laney and Matt. "They found him?"

"Yes, ma'am." Bonham pulled a small notepad out of his jacket pocket and handed it to the detective. She skimmed over the first few pages, leaving the others in the room holding their breath and fidgeting, then looked up at Bill, her eyes narrowed.

"There's nothing here about any apparent physical evidence?" Her question sounded like an accusation.

"No, ma'am. We didn't get that far. I was told to just take the initial statements and secure the area." Bonham shrugged.

"Well, if you're up for it, Bill, I could definitely use your help with this case. I'm only one person, and with a high-profile victim..." She glanced back at the body.

"We'll need to do a bunch of interviews," Bonham finished her sentence, nodding.

Laney watched the duo, feeling invisible and waiting to be questioned. As if the detective had read her mind, Worth turned to Laney and Matt.

"We're going to do our sweep of the scene first, then we'll follow up with more questions at a later date. I think for now your initial statements will do," she explained, dismissing them with a none-too-subtle glance at the door.

Laney decided not to push for more details just yet. She followed Matt outside, blinking like a mole venturing from his burrow when the stark light of day engulfed them. The golden sunshine was a depress-ingly dramatic contrast from the dark pall that had descended upon the interior of the house with the discovery of the mayor's body.

Roger sat, looking forlorn, on the porch steps, fidgeting with something that looked like a bobby pin. He was so focused on his mindless task, that he didn't even seem to notice when Laney sat down beside him. Matt went to his truck, then turned to gaze at the sad pair.

"Are you gonna be alright?" he called out, concern creasing his brow.

Roger lifted his head and waved. "We'll be okay, Matt. Thanks for asking."

Laney wasn't as confident about that, but she nodded anyway.

"Let me know if I can help." Matt gave them one last sympathetic glance before hopping into the mail truck and heading back down Maple Path. The gravel and dirt formed a hazy cloud in the truck's wake.

CHAPTER FIVE

After a quick sweep of the tea room, Detective Worth made note of the obvious physical evidence. There was an open window with a broken lock, which could be a sign of forced entry, provided that the window lock hadn't been broken before the incident. She added it to her list of questions for the interviews. With her phone, she took several photos of the floor by the sofa, for her own reference. Forensics would have a pro out to take their own photos, but Worth liked to keep some copies handy to study.

An untrained eye might have mistaken the scrapes that she'd spotted on the floor as simple everyday wear and tear, but after twenty-five years on the job, Worth could easily detect the new marks – marks that would be consistent with someone dumping a body in front of the sofa and making the legs scrape across the floor as it pushed back. The marks could indicate a struggle but weren't conclusive.

For the next hour, the detective scanned every inch of the room for less obvious clues, working around the forensics team, who was vacuuming, printing, and scooping up physical evidence that might give them an idea as to what had occurred. By the time she finished, she had pointed out and photographed several pieces of evidence that might prove helpful.

There had been a document sticking out of Mayor Andrew's jacket pocket, which was quickly identified as a copy of Marcy Dellin's will and there were several samples of hair on the front of the mayor's freshly pressed suit. Satisfied by the strong start, but determined to keep things moving along, Worth turned to Officer Bonham.

"Let's pack it up and give the team some room to do their thing. I want to talk to Miss Powers first, so you can head over to the post office to question Mr. Hall. I'll meet you back at the station and we'll go from there," she directed.

The detective found Laney sitting on the front steps

next to an older gentleman and cleared her throat to get the new tea room owner's attention. Laney and Roger glanced up at the sound, and both stood.

"Do you have some questions for me, Detective?" Laney asked, brushing off the seat of her jeans.

Worth's focus shifted to Roger.

"What's your name, sir?" she asked abruptly, startling the older man, who seemed surprised to be noticed.

"I'm Roger, ma'am," he said quickly, then hesitated.

"He's a family friend," Delaney offered. "My grandma Marcy - she used to own this place - was very close with Roger before she passed away a few months ago."

Roger nodded sadly.

"Marcy and I lived here for the past few years, but now Laney owns the tea room."

"Roger is welcome here as long as he likes." Laney placed a hand on his shoulder and squeezed gently.

Detective Worth made a mental note. She knew that the former owner had recently passed, and that her granddaughter had taken ownership of the tea room, but she found it odd that no one had mentioned the grandmother's boyfriend. She looked from Roger to Delaney - or Laney as he called her - trying to size them up. Though they didn't look suspicious in the least, Worth knew that everyone was a potential suspect until she had enough evidence to prove otherwise.

"Miss Powers, if you don't mind, I'd like to meet with you first," she told Laney, heading back into the house.

The detective seated herself at a small round table in the back corner of the main dining room and waited for Laney to take her seat before getting down to business.

Once the detective wrapped up her questioning, consulted with the coroner, and left, along with the forensics team, Laney was free to go about the rest of her day. Unfortunately, it seemed that her newly-acquired property had gathered a crowd. People stood on the sidewalk, chatting in groups of twos and threes, and speculating about what might have happened to the 'new kid' in town, so she'd have to wait until the crowd dispersed before she ventured out. She just wasn't mentally prepared to face the looks, the whispers, and the suspicions of her new neighbors. Iberden was such a placid, cozy place that anything requiring police presence brought even the most reticent residents out of their homes and into the street to see what had happened. People were curious. As annoying as it might be, Laney understood, and decided to just try to relax with a cup of tea until they lost interest and wandered away.

Laney had been looking forward to a peaceful start to her new life in Iberden, but the murder of the mayor had decidedly thrown a wrench into the works. She just wanted to take a break from her life in the city and escape her own personal drama, not get pulled into some sort of Nancy Drew nightmare.

Detective Worth had made it quite clear that Laney couldn't leave town until the investigation was closed. Though Worth's manner hadn't been overtly accusatory, Laney sensed that she'd been placed near the top of the suspect list, along with everyone she'd met so far in Iberden - Roger, Janet, Matt, and even dear old Babby. Humiliated that these outstanding citizens had been dragged into a mess, Laney felt quite sure that her fellow Iberden residents would be glad to see her head out of their content little hamlet just as soon as the case was closed, and that made her sad, not just for herself, but for her dear, well-intentioned grandma.

Detective Worth had at least mentioned that Laney and Roger could continue to reside in the tea room during the investigation now that the police were done gathering evidence from the crime scene. The parlor would be off limits for the time being, with barriers and yellow crime scene tape blocking the perimeter, but Laney was free to work on getting the rest of the tea room ready for customers, though the thought of the body that had been lying on the floor made her shudder every time she looked toward the parlor.

She was up in the air as to whether or not she'd actually have the skills and ability to successfully run a tea room. Perhaps it would be better left in the hands of someone more capable. Color flooded her cheeks when she remembered Marcy's note and she felt incredibly disloyal for even thinking of abandoning the gift from her grandma. It was almost like Grandma Marcy had known that something would happen to cause Laney to consider getting rid of the property.

At first, Laney had assumed that something had merely happened to the mayor for being in the wrong place at the wrong time, but the circumstances surrounding his death made her wonder. She felt like a heel now, for being so nasty to him the night before. True, he'd insulted her by patronizing her, and he'd seemed like a bit of a snake, but she shouldn't have been so rude. Grandma Marcy wouldn't have approved, she was quite sure of that.

Wrapping her arms around her midsection, standing in the foyer of her now-empty house, Laney had never felt more alone. She knew no one and trusted no one. Even in her anonymity in the city, she had never felt so bereft. Anyone that she'd met could've been a cold-blooded killer, though none of them seemed the type. The thought crossed her mind that she might be in danger herself, but she willed away those unhelpful thoughts. Right now, was a time to stay calm and move forward. She shook her head and took in a slow breath. She was on Detective Worth's suspect list at the moment, she could just tell, but in time, the detective would discover the truth and Laney's new life in Iberden could go on. She hoped.

CHAPTER SIX

The silence in the old Victorian house was deafening, so, once the crowds out front had moved on, Laney set off for the thrift store down the street, hoping for some distraction from the thoughts of the horrific events of the day. She made a mental note to find the grocery store while she was out. There was food in the refrigerator and in the cabinets, but it belonged to Roger, so she didn't feel right taking it.

Her first impression, once inside the thrift store, was that the collection of furniture that they featured was more contemporary and definitely more eccentric than what she had seen at Babby's.

"Laney?"

She heard a now-familiar voice call out from behind a massive oak bureau from the 70s. Matt stepped out into the aisle and raised a hand in greeting. "I had a feeling you'd be out scouting for things to furnish the tea room. Babby said you looked like a woman on a mission this morning."

"Well, honestly, after what happened at the tea room, I really needed to find something to do to keep my mind off of things." She sighed, wandering over to him and glancing at items along the way.

"Ahhh, they didn't clear you yet?" Matt asked.

Laney shook her head, unconsciously biting her lower lip.

"Me either, but don't stress - I think everyone knows who the real suspect is." He gave her a meaningful look.

"Umm…no, I actually have no idea." She frowned, her pulse accelerating.

"Oh, right. I forget, you're new around here, so you haven't heard all of the gossip. Miss Marcy wasn't one to share such things."

Matt paused, then looked around, as if verifying that there was no one lurking in the corners, eavesdropping. "There's Mayor Andrews' neighbor - he's had it out for him since the whole thing about moving his mailbox." He rolled his eyes. "The mayor kept telling the town clerk to refuse to approve the guy's permit to move his mailbox to the other side of the driveway."

Laney blinked, waiting for him to continue, entirely unsurprised to discover that the mayor hadn't been the world's best neighbor.

"Oh, and there's also that woman who was in charge of Marcy's will. I think her name's Janet?" he mused.

That got Laney's full attention.

"Really? She's the one who contacted me about the tea room." Laney frowned. "I figured she was just the attorney who handled Grandma Marcy's legal paperwork."

Matt shook his head. "Nope, she was apparently a family friend who moved here when Marcy's health started to decline. Janet was very protective of your grandma. She got into some heavy screaming matches with the mayor every time he tried to pressure Marcy to sell."

"Why did the mayor care so much about buying Marcy's Tea Room? He tried the same thing with me when I met him last night."

"Wait, Mayor Andrews was with you last night?" Matt's eyebrows shot skyward.

"I thought I was just meeting with Janet to go over the paperwork, but then Roger was there with her, and the mayor came in just as we were starting. He ended up sitting in on the meeting too, which I found odd, but I was kind of overwhelmed, so I didn't ask any questions." Laney shrugged.

"You told Detective Worth all this right?" Matt said slowly, looking at her strangely.

"Of course. Why wouldn't I?"

"Just wanna make sure the police have all the information," he replied, his eyes shifting away. "Anyway, good luck with your project." With a quick wave, Matt made a beeline out of the thrift store, leaving Laney with more questions than answers.

CHAPTER SEVEN

Laney wandered out of the thrift store empty-handed, replaying the conversation with Matt in her head, and wondering if she'd been foolish to tell him about her meeting with the mayor. Had she made herself a suspect in his mind? A wave of anxiety rolled through her, causing her stomach to clench. She was a newcomer in this tight-knit town. No one knew her, she had no friends, and she'd just made a very plausible case that pointed herself out as a viable suspect in the death of the mayor.

Matt had brought up Janet when he mentioned the obvious suspects, but now that Laney thought about it, he never got to explain why. Laney wondered if

Janet had been so protective of her grandmother that she be willing to do...anything to preserve her legacy. He'd also said that Janet was a family friend, so it was strange Grandma Marcy had never mentioned her. And stranger still that Janet hadn't mentioned it herself, at the reading of the will. Something fishy was going on, and Laney vowed to get to the bottom of it before the good citizens of Iberden chased her out of town with pitchforks.

She took out her phone and scrolled through her recent calls to find Janet's number. Staring at the screen for a moment, she considered calling or texting, but eventually thought better of it and slipped the phone back in her pocket. Her curiosity was killing her, but she decided that, for the moment at least, it would be best to leave the investigating to the police. They already looked at Laney with suspicion, she didn't want to do anything else that might put her in their sights.

The sun was just beginning to set as Laney reached 23 Maple Path, after stopping on the way home for some groceries. With a bag of groceries tucked under one arm, she unlocked the front door and turned on the lights as she walked into the main room.

"Roger?" Setting the groceries on the kitchen counter, she climbed halfway up the staircase to the upstairs living area, figuring she'd find him watching TV or reading. She stopped short when she noticed a few scraps of paper, that hadn't been there earlier in the day, littering the top steps.

Crouching down to pick up the pieces, Laney saw that it was her note from Grandma Marcy, torn into three crumpled pieces. Before she had dropped, exhausted, into bed last night she'd put the envelope with the note in the drawer of the nightstand, along with her copy of the will. Worried, she headed immediately to the guest bedroom and checked the nightstand. As expected, the drawer was empty. Her heart raced. What if it was the killer who had found the note? And what if she had been the intended victim, but the mayor came in at the wrong time and had to be eliminated?

Heart in her throat, Laney closed the nightstand drawer and stuffed the scraps of her letter into her pocket. She had to go to the police now. Her life might be on the line.

Detective Worth was sitting at the spare desk in Officer Bonham's office when the desk sergeant knocked on the door, with Laney in tow.

"Come in," she muttered, clearly distracted.

She closed the folder she'd been studying when she saw Laney. "Miss Powers. Can I help you?" Her expression was guarded.

"Please, call me Laney."

"Okay, then. Laney. Can I help you with something?" she repeated, her tone less than encouraging.

The detective gestured to the empty chair on the other side of the desk. Laney reached into her pocket, pulled out the scraps of paper, and placed them on the desk in front of Worth before taking her seat.

"I found this on the staircase at the tea room." Laney arranged the pieces so that Worth could read the message from her grandmother. "Did someone from your team search my room today?"

"Of course. Every room in the house was searched. Why?"

"I put this in the nightstand in the guest room last night. This morning when I left the house, it was still there, which means someone took it out of the nightstand and tore it to pieces. Whoever did it took my copy of Grandma Marcy's will, too. I found the torn up letter when I got back home, after your team investigated," Laney explained, her heart pounding.

"Well, I can assure you that if we had found the letter, we would have bagged it as evidence, so it had to have been taken before we got there," Worth replied. "We did find a copy of your grandma's will at the crime scene - it's currently in the evidence files. Can you certify that this is indeed your grandmother's handwriting?" She gestured to the pieces of Marcy's letter.

"Yes, it is." Laney nodded, her heart aching at the sight of the familiar scrawl. She'd seen it on every birthday card that she could remember.

Worth took a pair of tweezers and a plastic bag out of the case next to the desk and carefully picked up the pieces of the note, placing them in the bag. "It sounds to me like someone is trying to send you a message. I'll have Officer Bonham send an officer out to search the second floor this evening. If you see anything else out of the ordinary, be sure to let me know."

"I will."

The detective stared at her for a moment.

"Just make sure your doors and windows are locked and you should be fine."

Somehow, Laney was less than confident of that, but she put on a brave face and stood to go. A paper was sticking out of the folder in front of Worth, and before the detective reached out and flipped it over, Laney saw the name Raymond Andrews.

Was the mayor's name Raymond? Or was Raymond his next of kin? She couldn't put her finger on why but based on the detective's reaction when she saw Laney looking at the file, Laney made a point of remembering the name. Something told her that if she wanted to clear her own name, she was going to have to do some digging.

Determined to face her fears and get to the bottom of the murder that had happened in her dearly departed grandma's house, Laney trudged back down Maple

Path, hoping that she wouldn't find any other scary details when she reached the tea room.

CHAPTER EIGHT

"Alright," Officer Bonham said, coming down the stairs, "I think we're all set here."

"Did you find anything?" Laney asked.

The tech guys that he'd brought with him filed silently past Bonham on their way to the van.

"I'm not at liberty to discuss an ongoing investigation, Miss Powers."

He avoided her gaze, which made Laney nervous.

"Can you at least tell me if you found anything that makes it look like I might be murdered in my bed tonight?" she blurted, frustrated by his lack of response.

Bonham raised an eyebrow.

"Ain't no monsters under the bed if that's what you're asking. Have a good night," he replied dryly.

Roger had come in the door just as Bill and his team arrived, looking pensive and not saying much. It was understandable – he'd just lost his beloved. Laney's heart went out to the old man, and she didn't want to worry him, so she merely told him that the police were doing a follow up visit to make certain that they hadn't missed anything upstairs. He'd been quiet and morose since the mayor's body had been discovered and Laney didn't want to add to his burden by making him think that a killer might have been roaming the house earlier in the day.

Despite the exhaustion that descended upon her like a cold, dank cloud, when Laney locked the door after the police left, something nagged at her. The parlor was still blocked off, and Officer Bonham had made it clear that she was not to enter the area behind the tape, which made her wonder what might be in the parlor that she wasn't supposed to see. She hadn't so much as glanced around the room when Matt discovered the body, she was too busy calling for help. When she stopped to think about it, Laney realized that she didn't even know how the mayor was killed, having only seen his legs from behind the sofa.

A murder had taken place in her new home, and she knew nothing about it. Surely there wouldn't be any harm in just taking a look. After all, the police had had plenty of time to gather their evidence. Without giving herself time to change her mind, Laney marched over to the parlor, telling herself that as long as she didn't cross the barriers she wasn't technically doing anything wrong. The door to the parlor was closed and when she stood up on her tiptoes to peer inside through the window, the room itself was pitch-black.

With growing determination, she searched in a few places before finding a flashlight in the bureau drawer by the front door. Slipping quietly out the front door, Laney left it unlocked behind her as she hurried around the side of the house, coming to a stop in front of the parlor window. She switched the flashlight on and aimed the beam inside. The reflection on the window pane made it difficult to see so Laney leaned against the glass, never dreaming that the window would swing wide open with only a light touch, moving so fast that her arm scraped against the frame.

The lock that should have been on the window was completely gone. She hadn't heard anything drop inside when the window opened, but she did a quick check of the floor below to confirm that the lock hadn't just broken off during her little adventure, and sure enough the floor was clear of debris. Someone had obviously broken into the parlor. Was this how the mayor had entered, only to be followed by the killer, or had the killer merely used the tea room to dump the body and frame the new owner? Neither option made Laney feel any less sick to her stomach.

Before she pulled the window back in place, Laney glanced down at the interior wall and saw bright yellow marks on each side of the window. Somehow, that seemed noteworthy. Because she wasn't supposed to be anywhere near the parlor, she couldn't tell Detective Worth or Officer Bonham about her find, but surely there must be someone in whom she could confide and strategize.

Definitely not Matt. Despite the fact that he had shared a wealth of information with her, he clearly regarded Laney with suspicion. She wouldn't be surprised if telling him something like this might make him even more wary of her. Matt was someone she definitely wanted to keep in her corner. As Iberden's only mailman, he had to know all of the important gossip in town, which just might come in handy.

The next obvious person was Roger. If Grandma Marcy had trusted him, surely Laney could. She wished that her grandma had introduced them before she passed, but just knowing that the dear woman had someone who loved her during her last few years was enough for Laney. There was also the fact that Roger would probably be the only person who could confirm that the parlor window had, in fact, been closed and locked earlier this morning.

Walking back to the front of the house and entering the foyer, she resolved to speak with Roger in the morning, exhaustion descending upon her like lead weight. Still uneasy about returning to her bedroom, Laney lingered a bit, trying to decide how best to prepare for a killer who might come calling via the unlocked window in the parlor. There was a wooden chair in the guest room that she could wedge beneath the old-fashioned marble doorknob, and she kept the flashlight with her…just in case, as she trudged up to the guest room.

She hoped that Roger would be okay, since it was too late to disturb him, and when she crawled under one of her grandma's handmade quilts, she pulled the covers up to her neck and shivered. Despite the heaviness of her eyelids, it was quite a while before she dropped off to sleep, still listening for the creak of footsteps on the stairs.

CHAPTER NINE

"And then when I leaned on the glass, the window just kind of flew open," Laney explained to Roger, while the two of them munched on toasted English muffins with fresh creamery butter and orange marmalade.

"That doesn't surprise me," he replied, chewing a bite of English muffin slowly, then chasing it with a sip of tea. "The lock on that window has been broken for years. Your grandma and I were looking for an antique replacement lock that would match with the others in the house." He sighed, his eyes sad. "Searched all over the internet but apparently the company that made it shut down in the 50s. We looked in every antique and salvage store in the county and still haven't been able to replace it."

"I feel like that's an important detail. Do you think maybe we should mention it to the police?" Laney asked.

Roger looked up from his breakfast and blinked.

"I did mention it - to the detective. She wrote it down in her notebook during the questioning." Roger hesitated, then continued his explanation, "Worth told me not to discuss the details of the case with anyone - not even with you. That's why I haven't said anything to you about the whole unpleasant mess. I just assumed that she told you the same thing."

Laney's face flushed with heat. Of course, the detective told her not to discuss the case, but she'd taken for granted that Roger would tell her everything he knew.

"Yes, of course. I just thought that since we both live here now, and Grandma Marcy was so special to both of us..." She shrugged helplessly, feeling the ache of tears in the back of her throat.

"No worries. I think we both just need to toe the line a bit until they find the... person who did this foul thing."

"Sure, that makes sense," Laney murmured, buttering the last half of her English muffin, and avoiding his gaze.

She couldn't be angry with Roger for following the detective's orders, but she was embarrassed about oversharing and making a fool of herself. Now Roger knew what she had done, and she'd made it worse by showing him that she was willing to bend the rules when it was convenient, even during a murder investigation.

Roger cocked his head to the side and gazed at Laney pensively.

"You know..." he began, pouring another cup of tea and spooning sugar into it. "I'm not one to gossip, but you should probably know that there are actually a few people who had issues with the mayor."

"I know about the argument with his neighbor already," Laney confided. "Matt told me yesterday."

"I definitely don't think that was serious enough to prompt someone to murder." Roger shook his head. "But there *is* someone whom the mayor would've never imagined, who might've turned on him. Everyone in town, other than the mayor, knew what was going on. Maybe he was too blind to see it for himself, or maybe he just didn't want to."

Laney held her breath, waiting for Roger to continue. He seemed to consider his next words carefully before speaking again.

"You couldn't know this since you're new in town, but the mayor has a son, Raymond. Mayor Andrews adored that kid and had been grooming him his whole life to take over leadership of this town when he retired. What he hadn't anticipated was just how dangerous it can be to inspire that kind of ambition in someone who may not have the purest of motives. The truth is, the kid's been after his father's position for years, just chomping at the bit to replace him. That's what the buzz is in town anyway."

Roger shook his head. "Raymond's been schmoozing all the business owners and financiers in the state for years. We all knew it was only a matter of time 'til he phased his father out. That boy is mad for power.

Rumor has it that he isn't going to give up 'til he makes it to the Senate, at least."

Roger put down his teacup and placed his hand over Laney's on the table. "The point is, in my opinion, Raymond's the most likely suspect. And I'm telling you because I want to make sure you're careful about the people you get close to. He's a charmer, that one, but watch your back if he comes your way."

***

Laney's earlier conversation with Roger had been disconcerting to say the least, but also very illuminating. Her thoughts whirled as she walked to the cafe for a quick bite to eat before returning to the thrift store to look more closely at some of the items that she'd merely glanced at yesterday.

Despite the enormity of roadblocks in her way, given the current circumstances, there was no way that she was going to give up on her goal of restoring Marcy's Tea Room. Now that she had at least a little more information about the town, and specifically the people who had issues with the mayor long before she arrived, Laney felt more confident about the investigation. Surely, given enough time, the detective and Officer Bonham would figure out who would stand to benefit most from the mayor's death. The only puzzling thought that niggled in the back of her mind was...why had the killer dumped the body at the tea room? Could it have merely been an attempt to frame the new girl in town? Laney was hopeful that Detective Worth was smart enough to see right through that tactic if that had indeed been the killer's motive.

When she opened the door to the cafe, still lost in thought, Laney bumped into a man carrying out a to go box. He held the box above his head, to avoid dropping it on her, which she appreciated, but when she got a closer look at him, she nearly gasped.

Tall, broad, dark hair, and a winning smile. There was no mistaking the resemblance to Mayor Andrews.

"Sorry about that," Raymond Andrews said, seeming distracted. He chuckled, chagrined, and lowered the box back to chest-level. "Didn't see you there." He did a double-take. "You're not from around here," the mayor's son observed. "You must be visiting, because I'd definitely remember seeing you."

Roger had said that Raymond Andrews was a charmer. Even without the old man's advice, Laney was confident that she would've seen right through the oily smile that was so much like his father's.

"I'm Laney," she offered, forming her lips into a polite smile. It wouldn't do to make him suspicious.

"Raymond Andrews. Pleasure to meet you."

"Oh, you must be related to Mayor Andrews." Laney feigned innocence. "I'm so sorry for your loss."

"Thank you. Yes, I'm his son. You're the new owner of the tea room, right? I'm sorry you had to get dragged into a horrible mess."

"No apologies. I just hope that they find the person who did it soon, so they can bring them to justice."

"That makes two of us." Raymond nodded. "Not many people are offering their condolences these days. Most folks are behaving oddly. It's been…difficult. My dad was a great man. The bluster just hid his softer side." He swallowed hard and looked away. "I'm sorry." He shook his head. "It's just…all the gossip, the whispering - I know what they're saying. It doesn't make it any easier, that's for sure."

Laney had to work to keep her guard up, replaying Roger's warning about the mayor's son in her head.

She couldn't help but feel sorry for Raymond Andrews. His grief seemed entirely genuine, and she could definitely relate to feeling like the whole town was whispering and judging. Her name had probably been spoken by people in town more times than she was comfortable with, and for the same reasons.

"I know the feeling," Laney murmured, being honest and trying her best to remain neutral in the face of Raymond's evident sorrow.

"Well, enjoy your lunch." Raymond gave her a sad smile and hurried on his way, clutching his to-go box.

Laney watched him walk down Maple Path, more confused than ever. While she couldn't rule Ray out just yet as a suspect, his manner made her question her certainty. He wasn't the only suspect, and perhaps what she needed to do was explore the other possibilities a bit.

CHAPTER TEN

Laney sat down on a stool covered with cracked red vinyl at the counter of the café, mulling over her encounter with Raymond Andrews.

"Better watch out for that one," the ancient waitress who handed her a laminated menu counseled. "He's been known to be a heartbreaker."

"So I've heard," Laney mumbled, trying to focus on the menu. "Any favorites?" she asked, holding it up.

"The special is a hot turkey sandwich with stuffing and mashed potatoes. It comes with a drink and dessert. You won't leave here hungry with that one." The older woman chuckled, taking an order pad from the pocket of her bubblegum-pink uniform.

"That sounds perfect, thank you. I'll take the special, with coffee to drink, please." Laney smiled and handed her back the menu.

"You're welcome. I'm Irene. You just holler if you need anything," the waitress directed.

When she came back with a heaping plate of food, Irene eyed Laney intently.

"You're Marcy's granddaughter, aren't you?" she asked, with a fond smile.

"Yes, ma'am. I'm Laney."

"First time I saw you, you were about yea high." Irene held her hand roughly three feet from the floor. "Always a curious little thing. Your grandma loved you to the ends of the earth."

Laney's eyes misted for a moment, and she swallowed hard.

"I miss her," she admitted.

"I know, sweetie." Irene patted her shoulder. "We all do. I sure hope the police figure out what happened over at your place before too long." She shook her head. "Horrible thing."

"Yes it was. Any ideas?" Laney asked.

"One or two." Irene pursed her lips. "But not being a gossiping woman, I'm not going to say."

She leaned in and spoke in a low voice.

"Honey, just between you and me...I'd take a closer look at the people who were like moths to a flame when they heard that she was sick. Timing is everything."

"Irene...order up, please!" a voice called from the kitchen.

"That's me." She startled, her eyes wide. "Mind what I said."

Lancy watched her disappear into the kitchen, wondering. Like moths to a flame...who had come around when they heard that Grandma Marcy was ill? Roger? Janet? Neither of them seemed capable of murder. Lost in thought, she dug into her lunch, forking in turkey, stuffing, and mashed potatoes, slathered in gravy, much faster than she'd intended. She asked Irene, who said nothing more about the murder, to box up her peach cobbler to-go. The waitress disappeared after handing the cobbler to her, and Laney paid her bill, heading for the thrift store.

As luck would have it, there were two full sets of silver at the thrift store, and Laney snapped them up immediately, along with three silver tea pots, a cream and sugar set, and a shopping cart full of table linens.

"Wow, that's a lot of tablecloths," the teenage girl who was tending the cash register remarked, eyes wide.

"I have a lot of tables." Laney smiled absently. "I own Marcy's Tea Room."

The girl's china-blue eyes went wider still.

"Really? Are you like, totally freaked out right now?" she breathed.

"Yeah, a little bit, but I don't think I'm in any danger, so I just have to wait for the police to find whoever did it." Laney shrugged, the hairs on the back of her neck rising up at the girl's reaction.

"Are you still letting that old guy stay there?"

"Roger? Yes, of course. It was his home before my grandmother passed. Why wouldn't I let him stay?"

The teenager blushed.

"I shouldn't have said anything. Mama always says if I can't say something nice, I shouldn't say anything at all." She looked down and started scanning the tags on Laney's merchandise.

"I think it would be fine to talk about something that might help someone stay safe, don't you?" Laney asked.

"I suppose you're right." The teenager stopped in mid-scan, holding a teapot. "Please don't let anyone know that I said anything though…promise?" She glanced about, as though making certain that no one was near enough to overhear.

"I can't really make that promise without knowing what you're going to say," Laney admitted. "If you have information that will help solve a crime, I may have to share it."

The girl blinked a few times and played with the tail of one of her braids while she considered what to do.

"Well, it isn't information exactly. It's more like gossip." She shrugged.

"Then tell me and I'll let you know what I think."

"Okay, but if you tell someone, don't let them know that I said anything. Deal?"

"Deal." Laney nodded.

"So, I heard my mom talking to Mrs. Gardner when your grandma and the old guy started dating..." the teenager began, her eyes darting about the shop.

"Who is Mrs. Gardner?" Laney interrupted.

"Our next door neighbor. She used to play cards with your grandma and some other ladies. Anyway, Mrs. Gardner said that she thought that Roger was using Marcy as a meal ticket. Now, I don't know exactly what that means, but it didn't sound good, ya know?"

Laney nodded. "Go on..."

"After that they just said some things about how no one in town knows much about him, but the way they said it sounded, like, I don't know...kinda creepy, I guess."

"Like maybe he wasn't a good person?" Laney clarified.

"Yeah, like maybe he didn't actually care about your grandma. I don't know. Maybe Mrs. Gardner was just jealous or something. She's a widow, so maybe she was mad at Roger for asking Marcy out instead of her." The teenager shrugged again.

"Is that it?" Laney asked.

"That's all I can remember. It was a while ago, and when I came in the room, they kind of changed the subject."

"I see. And who is your mom?"

"You won't tell her I said anything, will you?" The girl bit her lip, looking guilty.

"Not at all."

"It's Willa Jean. She owns this store."

"And what's your name?" Laney smiled so that the teenager wouldn't think she was being interrogated.

"Carly."

"Carly, I'm Laney. It's been nice chatting with you, and your secret is safe with me."

Carly let out a breath.

"Oh, good. Thanks. Now, let me get these things rung up for you."

"Sounds good."

Laney left the store minutes later, her arms full of her purchases, her heart troubled by what she'd just heard.

It frustrated her that every time she returned to the tea room, she was halfway afraid to go inside. Climbing the porch steps anyway, Laney inserted her key in the lock and let herself in. It didn't feel like home yet. To be truthful, it didn't even seem like her tea room, but she was determined to get started on making it a cozy and charming place for guests to relax.

"Roger?" she called out when she stepped into the foyer.

The silence that she'd expected greeted her. Roger seemingly spent most of his time away from the tea room, and come to think of it, Laney never knew where he was at any given time. Not that he was accountable to her in any way – he was a grown man who could come and go as he pleased, it just seemed a bit odd that he hadn't stuck around to get to know Laney at all.

"Maybe it's just hard for him to be here, with all of the memories of Grandma all around him," she murmured to herself, setting down the heavy bags from the thrift shop against one wall, and stashing her to-go box of peach cobbler in the fridge. As sad as it seemed, she certainly hoped that was the case, and that there was nothing more sinister about Roger being gone all the time.

Laney had hatched a plan for fixing up the tea room one night recently, when sleep had eluded her. For starters, she was going to paint all of the beautiful Victorian trim in a fresh coat of white and change out the time-worn wallpaper. The chandeliers were beautiful, but the brass finish had to go, so she'd prime them and paint them white as well, and she planned to fashion cute little shades for them out of some of the colorful antique linens that she'd purchased. Once the walls and lighting were done, she'd paint the assortment of wooden chairs that she'd purchased with happy colors to coordinate with the wallpaper and rugs, covering the seats with fabric, and finally, once all of the messy work was done, she'd sand, and either stain or paint, the hardwood floors.

"No time like the present," Laney muttered, rolling up her sleeves and heading for the bag of tarps that she'd seen in the shed, out back.

Hard work was therapy, Grandma Marcy always said, and right about now, Laney could use a session or two.

CHAPTER ELEVEN

After hours of working on the tea room, Laney had just replaced the cover on the bucket of white paint when she heard a thump at the front door. Startled, she went absolutely still, listening. After a few minutes of hearing nothing out of the ordinary, she marched through the foyer and flung open the front door, ready to do battle with any boogeyman who might be on the porch. The fact that it was broad daylight, just before lunchtime, significantly bolstered her resolve.

She immediately saw the source of the sound. A rolled-up afternoon edition newspaper sat innocently on the welcome mat.

"Oh, my." Laney chuckled, shaking her head at her initial overreaction.

She picked up the paper and brought it inside. It was time for lunch anyway and reading the paper would help her pass the time while she ate, because, as usual, Roger was nowhere to be found.

Laney wanted to keep lunch simple, so that she could quickly eat and get back to work on the tea room. She whipped up a peanut butter and jelly sandwich and took giant bites of it while heating up the peach cobbler from the café in the microwave. When her dessert was warmed, she plopped it onto the plate next to her sandwich and headed for the small table in the main dining area that she and Roger had been using for their meals since she arrived.

When she took the rubber band off of her copy of the Iberden Chronicle, her eyes widened at the headline that screamed out at her: *One Shot Fired in Mayor's Murder!*

The Medical Examiner's findings had been released, along with a short statement from Detective Worth.

Laney pored carefully over every line of the story to make sure she had all the facts. In addition to revealing the cause of death, a gunshot, the article made a vague reference to pressure, coming from law enforcement at the state level, to wrap up the investigation as quickly as possible, which Laney found odd. Why would state representatives care about a murder case in a tiny town like Iberden? Detective Worth was quoted as being 'optimistic that the case would close very soon."

The article gave no details about the investigation, the crime, or a potential motive, leaving Laney with far more questions than answers. She was fairly certain that nearly everyone in town had probably read the article and she expected to hear talk of it throughout the day, once she went out and about. She couldn't really blame the townies. The mayor's murder was undoubtedly the biggest and most awful event that had ever made the news in Iberden.

When she turned the page, Laney saw the announcement for Mayor Andrews' funeral, which would take place later this afternoon.

Her phone rang, and Laney's heart nearly stopped when she saw Detective Worth's number on the caller ID.

"Laney speaking," she answered, trying not to sound as rattled as she felt.

The detective asked her to come to the station, and, glancing at her watch, Laney promised to be there in ten minutes. Worth said a curt goodbye and the line went dead, leaving Laney with a dark dread curling in her stomach.

Trying to be optimistic and hoping that the detective wanted to give her the good news that Mayor Andrews' killer had been caught, Laney grabbed her purse and strode down Maple Path at a brisk pace, so lost in thought that she didn't even notice Roger waving at her until she heard him calling out to her from across the street.

"Laney!" He made his way across the street, hurrying toward her.

She thought about ignoring him and continuing on, which of course made her feel guilty, but decided to stop, for just a moment. She didn't want to be late to see Detective Worth.

"Where are you off to in such a hurry?" he asked, a bit out of breath.

After yesterday's conversation, Laney wasn't sure how much she should tell him, but decided on the spot that it shouldn't hurt to let him know where she was going. She could honestly say that she didn't even know why the detective had asked to see her.

"Detective Worth wanted to see me."

"You, too?" His eyebrows rose. "First Matt, then Raymond, then Janet, then me, and now you. She must be running down the whole list this morning." He looked at Laney quizzically.

"Interesting." Laney frowned. "Well, I guess it's my turn - better get going."

The thought crossed her mind that Roger might wait for her outside, but when she reached the front of the police station, she saw him continue toward the tea room without so much as a backward glance.

Detective Worth was jotting down some notes when Laney was led to her desk by the same sergeant who had brought her in the first time. Checking the clock on the wall, Laney was relieved to see that, despite her encounter with Roger, she was still right on time.

"Come in." The detective flipped to a fresh page on her notepad and gestured to the chair on the other side of the desk.

Once Laney was seated, she gazed at Worth, trying not to fidget. The detective unexpectedly gave her a brief, polite smile, and Laney had to wonder whether it meant that she should be relieved, or that she should prepare herself for a night in jail. Surely the detective wouldn't be so callous as to smile at her before arresting her..

"I called you down because you've officially been cleared." Worth seemed to study her closely when she made the proclamation.

Laney tilted her head back and closed her eyes for a moment, sagging with relief. She drew in a deep calming breath and opened her eyes.

"Thank you," she murmured, finding it odd that the detective was watching her like a hawk. "So, what happens now?" Laney gathered her composure and sat up straight.

"I just need to ask you a few more questions," Worth replied, her tone neutral.

She opened her notebook, flipped through a few pages and studied it for a moment.

"Janet O'Shea arrived in Iberden almost exactly a year ago. Based on my interviews with local residents, she reportedly came to help take care of her family friend, Marcy Dellins."

Laney's expression was blank as she waited for the detective to continue.

"Had you ever met, or even seen, Ms. O'Shea before the night you came to get the paperwork for your grandmother's will? Did you recognize her at all?"

"No." Laney frowned, thinking. "I received the letter from her that morning about the tea room and came on the first bus that would get me here. I had no idea who she was and didn't even know she had any sort of relationship with Grandma Marcy. I thought she was just the attorney who handled my grandma's will, honestly." Laney paused, seeming to reconsider her last answer. "Wait, that's not exactly correct," she amended hastily, wanting her answers to be as accurate as possible.

Worth raised her eyebrows and waited for Laney to continue.

"The next day, Matt told me that she was a family friend, but he didn't say much else about her."

"I see." The detective made a note. "Have you seen Janet since the night you arrived in Iberden? Do you know her current whereabouts?"

Laney shook her head, eyes wide. "Why, is she missing?"

Worth let the question hang in the air unanswered, then moved on.

"Last question - when you met with Janet and the others, was she carrying anything?"

"She had her purse hanging on the back of the chair... but I didn't see her carrying anything unusual."

Laney watched as Worth circled something on her notes page, then closed the book and stood up, indicating the end of the interview.

"That's all for now. Thanks for coming down here so quickly." Worth led Laney out of the station. "I might reach out again soon," she advised. "We're getting there, but we need to tie up all the loose ends before we close the case."

"That's good news." Laney smiled, feeling shaky.

"I hope so," the detective replied cryptically.

CHAPTER TWELVE

Laney had assumed that she'd feel much more relieved than she actually had, when the detective notified her that she'd been cleared as a possible suspect. She was grateful, but she couldn't ignore the questions the kept rising in her mind, urging her to keep digging.

Worth seemed most suspicious about Janet O'Shea, but Lancy wondered if she had deliberately brought up Janet in order to throw her off of the real focus of the investigation.

According to Roger, Raymond Andrews had the most obvious motive, even though he'd seemed like a truly grieving son when she ran into him at the cafe.

She tried to imagine how obsessed by hatred, greed, and jealousy someone would have to be to commit such a crime, which oddly led to thoughts of her own family. Her mom and dad basically disowned her when she dropped out of business school years ago, but she'd never consider hurting them, ever, and she knew that the thought of inflicting physical harm would never cross their minds either.

It also seemed like Raymond, the son that the mayor was so proud of, would stand to lose everything he'd ever worked for if he got caught, so why would he take the chance? The more she thought about it, the less and less likely it seemed that the man she ran into in the cafe would be inclined to do such a thing. Even though Roger warned her about him, Laney just couldn't buy into the thought of him as the culprit.

She also found it strange that apparently, Janet had disappeared. Janet may have been the last person to see the victim alive. Had she simply been so horrified when she heard the news, that she'd left town? Or had she been so grief-stricken after Marcy's death that she left after the meeting, never to return. There was a possibility that Janet O'Shea might not even know that a murder had taken place in Iberden.

A realization struck Laney just then. A realization so profound that it had her practically sprinting back to the tea room, where she grabbed her suitcase from the closet and tossed it onto her bed.

"I know it's in here somewhere," she muttered, digging through clothing and toiletries.

She unzipped the semi-hidden pocket in the bottom of the bag and reached inside, her fingers touching crinkled paper. Pulling out the original letter that Janet had sent her and flattening it on a spot on the floor where she was currently squatting, her eyes flew to the bottom, where Janet had signed and noted her personal cell number in case of an emergency. It would have been very strange for Janet to offer Laney this number if she was somehow involved in the murder. This piece of crumpled paper might just help exonerate Grandma Marcy's mysterious friend.

Laney headed back to the police station with the letter tucked carefully into her pocket. She didn't pass anyone on Maple Path, which she found curious at first, but when she checked the time she remembered that the mayor's funeral had been scheduled to start a few minutes ago.

She entered the station and stopped at the front desk,

but when she told the sergeant that she was looking for Detective Worth, the uniformed woman shook her head.

"The detective isn't in at the moment. Would you like to leave her a message?"

"Oh." Laney thought for a moment. "Uh, no. No thank you...I'll just catch up with her later."

Following a hunch, she hurried toward the most logical place where she just might find the detective.

It wasn't difficult to discover the location of the mayor's funeral, when nearly all the townspeople were gathered behind one of the six churches in town. Laney had simply looked for a bunch of parked cars and the rest had been easy. She stood a respectful distance away from the ceremony and scanned the crowd for Detective Worth. She spotted the detective right away, just on the other side of the lawn.

Worth's eyes were focused on Raymond who stood by the priest. Though his face was a mask of solemnity, Raymond's eyes darted from left to right and back again, taking in the congregation, but always returning to the detective. His attention was drawn back to the funeral when the casket was lowered into the ground. Raymond shoveled a ceremonial bit of earth into the hole, his expression grave.

When the final prayers were said, Laney ducked behind the corner of the church to keep out of sight, waiting for people to leave, her gaze roaming the empty streets of Iberden.

She heard the murmurs of the crowd as they shuffled toward their cars and homes, and peeked around the corner, looking for Detective Worth. It wasn't until everyone else had left the area that she was able to spot the detective talking to Raymond. She didn't want to intrude on their conversation, but she knew that she had to give the detective the letter from Janet. Worth and Raymond both had their backs to Laney and were so engrossed in their conversation that they didn't see or hear her as she approached

"I'm sorry," Worth insisted, her eyes flicking momentarily to the cemetery crew, who had begun the process of filling in Mayor Andrews' grave. "I know this is a difficult time, but you need to come to the station and answer some more questions."

"I told you everything I know." Raymond voice was

hoarse and sounded like he was barely holding back tears. "What more do you want?"

"There's new evidence that suggests you know more than you've shared."

Laney froze in place, the letter clutched in her hand.

The detective continued, "You can either come willingly, or I can parade you to my car in handcuffs, if that's what you'd prefer. Obstruction of justice is a very real charge, Mr. Andrews, and it could ruin a political career."

Laney saw Raymond run a shaky hand over his forehead.

"Fine." He shook his head, finally.

"Are you okay with walking?" Worth asked.

"Do I have a choice?" Raymond shot back.

Laney quickly backpedaled, ducking behind some bushes near the side of the church, hoping desperately that neither Worth nor Raymond had spotted her. Her heart thrummed so loudly in her chest that she worried they'd hear it as they walked by on their way to the police station.

Apparently, despite the fact that the detective had only asked questions about Janet O'Shea, Raymond Andrews was still the primary suspect. Glancing down at the crumpled paper in her hand, Laney felt torn, wondering what she should do next.

The rational side of her told her to go back to the tea room and leave well enough alone, but her quest for the truth and for closure, spurred her on. Knowing that Worth would be tied up with questioning Raymond for at least a little while, Laney vowed to find Janet. She believed the woman was innocent and hoped that she might have some answers. Decision made, her fingers moved across her phone's keypad, dialing the number written at the bottom of the note that had already managed to change her life.

CHAPTER THIRTEEN

There was no answer the first several times that Laney had tried to call Janet, so she went back to home to try and organize her thoughts. Having gotten nowhere, Laney tried calling again. When she finally answered on the third ring, her voice trembled.

Laney's heart sank to her knees when she realized that she might just be speaking with a cold-blooded murderer. She shivered, despite having climbed into bed, huddling under the warmth of Grandma Marcy's quilt. It was draped over her knees as she sat up, leaning against the antique headboard of her bed, though it was only 4:30 in the afternoon.

"Janet, it's me - Laney," she half-whispered into the phone. If Roger was in the house, there was no need for him to know about this call.

There was a brief moment of silence, then Laney heard Janet let out a long breath.

"Thank goodness," she replied. "Are you okay?"

It was an odd question, and Laney wondered what had prompted it.

She decided to ignore the question and dove right in, before she could come to her senses and change her mind.

"I need to talk to you," Laney said, still in a hushed voice. "You know what's going on here in Iberden, don't you?"

"Of course, I know," Janet snapped, then softened her tone a bit. "I can't say anything right now, but I'll text you my address when we hang up. Come as soon as you can - I think it's time to tell you the truth."

That simple word...truth...hit Laney right in the gut, like a sucker punch. She didn't know what truth Janet was talking about, but it certainly didn't sound pleasant. Her suspicion growing by leaps and bounds, she blurted out a question in an attempt to keep Janet on the line and hopefully get some answers.

"Where are you?"

For a moment, Laney heard nothing but the faint rise and fall of Janet's breathing. Finally, she spoke, sounding more than reluctant.

"I'm at my home. I live in the next town over. Please, tell me you'll come soon."

Laney response was immediate. "Text me the address now."

She hung up, and roughly ten seconds after she ended the call, her phone vibrated with Janet's message. Checking the map app, Laney confirmed that she'd have to find a way to make it three miles west to Janet's location. She didn't have a car, and seriously doubted that there would be a bus between the two towns that late in the afternoon.

The only person that she could halfway trust, who had a vehicle and might be willing to help her out on such short notice was Matt. Now that she officially wasn't a suspect, maybe he'd be more likely to give her a hand.

If she sprang into action right away, Laney might be able to catch Matt before he left work. Practically leaping from the bed and grabbing her purse as she slid her feet into her shoes, she left the house and headed down Maple Path at a rapid pace, hoping she could convince the mailman to give her a ride.

The bell above the door jangled when Laney entered the post office at 4:58pm. When she saw Matt walk in from the back room, she smiled shyly and waved. Grandma Marcy always said you could catch more flies with honey, and she needed this particular fly to drive her three miles away, so she poured it on.

"Hey, Laney." He greeted her with a puzzled smile. "What're you doing here?"

"Actually, I was looking for you." She hesitated, but knew she had no time to lose. "I know this is random, but can you give me a ride?" she blurted, pleading with her eyes.

"Ummmmm…" Matt seemed to be trying to formulate an acceptable excuse, but Laney was willing to beg at this point.

"I just need to get over to a friend's place in Brigton. It's only a short drive. I'd walk but I'm kind of in a hurry. Please, Matt, you're the only person that I can trust in this town. I don't know anyone else well enough, and you seem honorable. I'll make it up to you somehow, I promise."

Matt's face flushed scarlet, and he fidgeted, scratching his ear, and shifting from one foot to the other while Laney stared at him. Seconds ticked by and just when Laney was so frustrated that she thought she might scream if he didn't answer her soon, Matt caved.

"Okay." He sighed, grabbing his keys from the front desk. "Let's go."

They drove by Centennial Woods, a stretch of tall trees that formed the border between Iberden and Brigton. While Iberden was a small town, it was condensed - the shops and houses were rather close together and it seemed likely that a person would call out the window to their neighbor just to say, "good morning."

Things were different on the other side of the woods. The few homes she saw were separated by fields of grass that covered enough area to contain several more houses. In no time at all, with Laney dictating instructions, Matt's pickup truck came to a stop in front of the small cottage on the edge of the woods.

"This is it, right?" Matt asked, staring at the house.

Those were the only words he'd spoken during the entirety of the short ride and Laney hoped that his silence hadn't been because she'd upset him by being slightly manipulative.

She referred to the text message she had saved - 205 Centennial Ct, Brigton VT. A quick look at the number on the mailbox confirmed that they were in the right place.

Laney nodded and thanked Matt before getting out of the truck. She had barely closed the door when he pulled away, his skidding tires leaving a dusty cloud behind. He seemed a bit miffed, but Laney didn't have time to dwell on the mailman's feelings at the moment. She'd apologize tomorrow, but for right now, her focus was solely on talking to Janet.

It was still light outside, though the sun was starting to set. Walking up wooden steps to the hand-hewn logs that composed the front porch, Laney began to question her decision to come here, particularly since Matt had left in such a hurry. Out here in the sticks, no one would even hear her scream. Shivering, she shook off her fear. She had a job to do, and right now, that job was to get as much information as possible out of the woman who had been her grandmother's friend.

Laney stood waiting silently after rapping on the heavy front door, straining to hear what the voices on the other side of it were saying.

"She's here," Laney heard.

She couldn't identify the voice, but she knew that it didn't sound like Janet. It sounded like a man. She heard the sound of footsteps approaching the door, getting louder as they got closer. The knob turned, and like something out of a horror movie, the door slowly creaked open.

Much to her surprise, Laney saw Janet and Roger side by side. The duo gazed past her, as though they were expecting company, then exchanged a look. Roger shook his head and Janet sighed with relief.

"You didn't bring the police," Janet commented.

"Why would I do that?" Laney asked, being deliberately cagey.

She was alone and outnumbered. She wasn't about to take any chances.

"Please," Roger beckoned. "Come in." Laney followed the two inside to the dining room table, images of her first night in town flashing through her mind.

Once seated, Janet turned to Roger. "Grandpa," she addressed him, causing Laney's jaw to drop. "Do you want to start explaining or should I?"

CHAPTER FOURTEEN

Laney stared, speechless, at Janet, then at Roger, and back at Janet again. She hadn't known what to expect, but it certainly hadn't been anything like what she'd just heard.

Roger spoke softly, first looking down at his hands, then gazing up at Laney, a faraway look in his eyes. "I think this is my story to tell. Laney, I'm so sorry you got dragged into all this, but you deserve to know the truth."

Laney had a million questions whirling through her mind, but the most pressing one is what came out.

"What did you do?" she whispered, swallowing hard.

Inexplicably, Roger's eyes filled with tears. Janet

covered his hand with hers on the table, comforting him.

Laney folded her arms and stared at him. "Just start at the beginning," she said dully.

There was an awkward silence, while Roger's mouth worked as he tried to form the words, then Janet spoke.

"Do you want some tea?" she asked softly.

Laney nodded, dazed. Tea. Why not? This whole mess had something to do with her grandma's tea room. Perhaps it was appropriate to drink tea while trying to muddle through it. The bracing liquid might even help bring some clarity to the jumbled mass of questions and suspicions in her brain.

Janet rose from her seat. "I'll be right back. You just listen to his story," she directed.

When Janet left the room, Roger cleared his throat a couple of times and finally began to speak. "Your Grandma Marcy loved you so much," he murmured, staring at Laney with a look that she couldn't quite decipher. "I never thought for a minute that she would have waited for so long to tell you about us. I figured you'd know as much about us as we do about you. I was so looking forward to your visit in November."

Laney's eyes filled with unshed tears as she recalled the plans that she and Grandma Marcy had made for her visit, this coming November. But that had been before she had been diagnosed with cancer. It had been before they discovered that dear Marcy had only weeks to live. Struggling with trying to make ends meet, Laney wanted to visit, but hadn't been able to scrape up the money in time. She'd mightily regretted not being there for her grandma's last days, and if she had it to do all over again, she was quite sure she would've begged, borrowed or stolen to get to her grandma – just to see that dear face one last time, and tell her how much she loved her.

A lone tear trickled down her cheek and Roger resumed his story.

"When Marcy passed, Janet and I wanted so much to talk to you, but we thought it'd be best for you to the be the one to initiate the conversation. We didn't want to overstep." Roger looked down at a spot on the wide pine floor. "We figured when you didn't call, that you were too upset to talk to us, so we kept our distance.

That is, until Janet needed to reach out to you about the tea room."

He raised his gaze and stared into Laney's soul. "Janet told me you sounded confused when she talked to you, but again, we thought you were just grieving - that when you arrived in Iberden we could finally meet in person and things would be different."

Laney frowned, wondering exactly what Roger was getting at. She flashed back to her first day in Iberden and remembered seeing the disappointment in his face when she admitted she didn't know who he was. That memory made what he was saying much more understandable, though she knew that there were some key bits of information that he was keeping from her.

"When I finally understood the situation, I didn't want to shock you with too much information at once, so I held back. I figured that finding out I was supposed to marry your grandma was enough of a surprise. You didn't need to deal with hearing about how my own granddaughter was helping care for Marcy during those final days."

Roger's words came out in a rush, like a dam that had suddenly burst, and Laney felt compassion for the soul-battered old man in front of her. They sat in silence for a bit, each thinking their own thoughts.

Replaying the events from the past few days in her mind, Laney realized why Roger and Janet kept their relationship a secret after the murder.

"You didn't want to give anyone a reason to suspect Janet," she murmured. "You were protecting her, just like you tried to protect me."

Roger nodded solemnly.

"Janet didn't do anything wrong, but I knew she'd gotten into some arguments with Mayor Andrews before. Seemed like she was always trying to keep Marcy from being manipulated into selling the tea room. Since Marcy passed, my Janet is all I have left. I would do anything I could to keep her safe. And you, too, of course," he added, reaching over to briefly cover Laney's hand with his.

Laney was so overcome by gratitude - both for Roger and Janet - that she didn't even notice Janet placing a steaming cup of tea next to her.

"Thank you," Laney said softly, looking from one to the other. "Thank you both for loving my grandmother and taking care of her when the wolves were at her door. It should have been me taking care of her, but since I couldn't..." She paused and wiped a tear from her cheek. "I'm glad that you two were there for her."

"I just did what was right," Janet said simply. "Grandpa's the closest thing I have to a father, and he loved Marcy so, so much." Her voice quavered and she took a breath. "When he called me in the spring to ask to help him take care of her, I dropped everything and moved into the tea room that very day."

"Does anyone in town know you're related?" Laney wondered aloud. "I know when I talked to Matt the other day he said you were a family friend."

Janet and Roger exchanged a glance.

"I don't think anyone ever bothered to ask," Janet replied. "We weren't hiding it from anyone, but I didn't want any part in the town gossip, so I just kept to myself - other than the confrontations with Mayor Andrews." She shrugged.

"So, it's possible that Matt knew," Roger supplied. "Which only serves to underscore the reasons why we couldn't tell any of this to Detective Worth. Think about how it would have looked."

Laney couldn't argue with that. She could only imagine how Worth might have reacted upon discovering that Roger and his secret granddaughter - who also happened to have had several confrontations with the mayor - were the last ones to see Mayor Andrews alive.

Laney sighed and uttered the words that they were surely all thinking. "What a mess."

"And now we're so far into the lie, I don't even know how to get out of it." Janet shook her head, tears streaking down her cheeks. She impatiently dashed them away. "That's why Grandpa told me to stay away from Iberden, and now the whole thing has just turned into a twisted set of circumstances."

Laney's heart went out to Janet and Roger, but, as she saw it, there was only one way out of their predicament.

"We need to go to Worth," she declared.

Janet opened her mouth to argue, but Roger spoke first.

"That's why I came here, to get Janet," he explained. "So, I can bring her back to Iberden. I'll tell Worth this was all my fault, even if that gets me added back to the suspect list…and even if I have to face jail time for lying."

Laney admired Roger's courage, but she wasn't about to just let him give up.

"I'm coming with you," she insisted, throwing caution to the wind. "I'll vouch for you and maybe, once everything is out in the open, we'll be able to find evidence that proves Janet's innocence."

"Just how do you propose we do that?" Janet quirked an eyebrow at her.

"I have no earthly idea. We'll just have to think of something." She took Janet's hands. "You're not going down for this." She turned her gaze to Roger. "And neither are you. After everything you've done for me and Grandma Marcy, we're family. I may not have been here when Grandma Marcy needed me, but I'm here now, and we're going to get through this together."

CHAPTER FIFTEEN

Janet, Laney, and Roger entered Detective Worth's office en masse, presenting a unified front. Worth merely reacted to Laney and Roger's appearance with a raised eyebrow, but when her eyes met Janet's, her expression changed from benign disinterest to an almost predatory glare. Laney stepped forward, ready to speak for all three of them, and commanded the detective's attention with a steady gaze.

"We need to talk," she said quietly.

Laney relayed every detail of what she'd learned from Roger and Janet, not leaving anything out. She knew that if she left one iota of the story out, and Worth found out about it, the futures of all three of them might be in jeopardy. She finally finished her in-depth explanation, with Roger and Janet standing silently behind her, their postures a bit more relaxed. At this point, they'd done the right thing, and it was all they could do. What the detective chose to do with the information was entirely up to her. Worth folded her arms and regarded the trio thoughtfully.

"From a legal standpoint, I actually can't press charges because nothing that either of them did crosses the line into criminality. I'm not saying that I believe the whole story, but that's neither here nor there at this point. The case is close to wrapping up and all of you have been cleared."

Laney thought of Raymond and the thought of Worth arresting him just didn't sit well with her. Unless he's a better actor than she realized, his grief had been genuine. Had he merely been sad and scared about the possibility of getting caught? The scene that had played out between him and the detective seemed to almost support that theory. Almost. While relieved that Janet and Roger were no longer on the detective's watch list, Laney couldn't help but think that maybe the mayor's son had some skeletons in his closet, but not the ones that Worth thought he had.

The detective ushered them out of the office and the trio headed back to the Tea Room. They crowded into the cab of Janet's truck, and she drove them the short distance, even though it was an easy walk. After the ordeal that they'd all endured, confessing their omissions to each other as well as to a homicide detective, it just made sense that they wanted to stick together for a bit, catching their breath in companionable silence.

Laney offered Janet the use of the pullout couch in the second guest room when they got back. It wasn't fancy, but it would do. Having lost all sense of time, and running on sheer adrenaline, Laney only realized that it was after midnight when she saw Roger and Janet yawning as they trudged into the foyer and headed immediately upstairs. She heard doors closing behind them as they got settled in, but even after changing into her nightgown and slipping under the covers, sleep eluded her. Her eyes stared sightlessly at the ceiling, her mind whirling.

Just after she'd counted a hundred sheep for the third time, Laney suddenly sat straight up in bed and switched on her lamp. Someone had rapped lightly at the front door. With a killer still at large, at least for now, she wondered, heart pounding, who on earth would just show up out of the blue and knock on the door after midnight?

One realization pulled her racing pulse back to nearly normal limits...killers don't knock.

Quickly tossing on a sweatshirt and yoga pants, Laney raced down the stairs to open the door before whoever had been so inconsiderate could wake Roger and Janet.

You could have knocked her over with a feather when she saw Raymond Andrews standing on her front porch.

"I know it's late. I'm sorry, but I really need your help," he pleaded in a low voice.

Trying her best not to tremble as she stood facing a man who may or may not have murdered his own father in cold blood, Laney gaped at him for a moment, unsure as to how she should respond.

"I'm sorry, I don't understand," she replied truthfully.

"I know you have every reason to slam the door in my face, but all the awful things that people are saying about me just aren't true, and I really think that some-how...you know that. The way that you look at me and listen to what I have to say is so refreshing. There's no history or rumors clouding your perspective. Sometimes being born and raised in a small town can be pretty brutal, when folks make you a target." He sighed.

Laney chewed on her lower lip, weighing his words. He seemed genuine, just like he had every time she'd seen him, but Roger's warning still echoed in her mind, and Detective Worth's skepticism had been evident.

Raymond seemed to register her doubt and grimaced, before taking a deep breath and speaking again. "Listen, if you help me…I can prove to you that I'm not the man everyone thinks I am." His eyes locked with hers, pleading. A muscle twitched at his jaw.

"How?" Laney asked, at a loss.

Raymond seemed to deflate a bit, with every trace of his usual bravado gone.

"Honestly, I have no idea, but what I do know is that I didn't do this, so there's gotta be some sort of clue as to who did. I have some suspicions, but I need to follow up on them, and I need someone in my corner while I do."

He looked at her so hopefully that Laney's expression softened. If he was a liar, he was a darn good one... which is almost exactly what Roger had said. Deciding to trust her gut, she chose, for the moment at least, to believe that Raymond was innocent, and hoped that his request for help wasn't just a ploy to gain her confidence so that she could become his next victim.

She glanced over her shoulder, toward the stairs, hoping that Roger and Janet were still asleep and wouldn't come down. Raymond picked up on her distracted look.

"Janet and Roger are here, aren't they?" he asked. How would he know Janet is there?

Laney nodded. "Yeah, we've all had a rough time of it lately."

"I get that," Raymond replied. "You can tell them I'm here if you want, but we both know how they'll react. Just let me explain everything to you first, then you can decide if you want to bring them in on it. Fair enough?" he asked, eyebrows raised.

"Fine," Laney agreed. "But any talking that we need to do will be done here, with them sleeping upstairs," she insisted.

Raymond's face fell. "You don't trust me. I suppose you're smart to be careful like that, and I don't blame you at all. Talking here is fine with me. Thank you for the chance to explain."

Laney stepped aside to let Raymond into the foyer, and he followed her to the table that she and Roger had been using for their meals. It was far enough from the stairs that they wouldn't have to whisper. They could speak normally and not have to worry about waking up Roger and Janet, but they were close enough that a scream from Laney would bring them running.

They took a seat across from each other and Laney placed her elbows on the table, clasping her hands under her chin, ready to listen.

CHAPTER SIXTEEN

"I know you were there, behind the church today, after the funeral," Raymond offered, gazing at her without judgement.

Laney contemplated denying it, but really what would be the point?

"Yes, I was there," she admitted, squirming in her chair. "But I really didn't hear much at all," she added.

Raymond nodded. "That part doesn't even matter, actually, I'm just confirming that you know the background info - that Detective Worth questioned me today." He waited for Laney to nod before continuing.

"She found something when she was going through

my dad's financial records." He paused and took a deep breath. "Apparently there was a lot of money coming out of his bank account every month, for as far back as she could pull." Laney frowned, not grasping how all of that pertained to Raymond, but she listened intently when he continued. "Our accounts are linked." He dropped the bombshell.

"So, it looks like you've been stealing money from your father...or maybe even blackmailing him or something?" Laney breathed, her jaw dropping.

Raymond dropped his head into his hands in frustration, then rubbed his face angrily before looking up again.

"See? That's the problem. With just that one piece of "evidence," that's the first conclusion that everyone jumps to. Even the detective, and she should know better," he hissed, exasperated. "I can't even really be mad at her for blaming me after that. I mean if I was her, I'd probably blame me too, but the fact remains that I didn't do any of that."

He pushed back his chair and stood up, pacing back and forth through the main room, his footsteps echoing in the stillness of the tea room. "Dad was always the one in charge of the finances. I never handled any of the financial stuff. I was the logistics man - I dealt with all of the town planning, business, and social events. I stayed in my lane; that's how we functioned so efficiently for the past eight years."

Raymond ran his hands through his hair, tousling it in a way that made him look almost boyish. "Obviously Worth isn't going to take my word for it. I swear, Laney, I didn't know anything about the money. I still don't know what all of those withdrawals are about."

"That's a horrible position to be in, but I don't understand, what do you think I can possibly do to help? I don't even know you, and I'm the new kid in town, so no one will listen to me anyway." Laney shrugged helplessly.

They both stopped speaking and turned when they heard footsteps descending the stairs. Roger and Janet reached the bottom and stood, arms crossed, and eyes narrowed at the uninvited midnight visitor.

Laney stood and put her hands up to silence the objections that they were undoubtedly about to make. "It's okay. I let him in."

Roger, old though he may be, locked eyes with the younger man, his hands clenched into fists at his sides. Janet put a hand firmly on his forearm and gave him a warning look. If Raymond Andrews was indeed dangerous, any fight that Roger tried to put up wouldn't end well for him.

Trying to defuse the situation and smooth some very ruffled feathers, Janet interrupted the death glares that the two men were giving each other, trying to serve as peacemaker.

"So, what's the news?" she asked, as though it was perfectly normal to have the dead mayor's son standing in the tea room in the wee hours of the morning.

She slowly released her hold on Roger's arm when the older man had settled a bit. "I'm assuming we're supposed to believe he's innocent?" she asked, nodding at Raymond, her tone matter-of-fact.

Raymond actually chuckled.

"Yes, please. I *am* innocent, and I came here because I thought that you and Laney would be able to help me prove it."

Janet blinked taken aback. "Me?" Her eyebrows shot skyward, while Roger pursed his lips beside her. "How could I possibly help you with that?"

"You're far more knowledgeable about how the legal system works than I am."

"Seriously?" Janet shook her head. "You want me to help you get off on a technicality? Forget it."

"Last I heard, innocent people didn't need technicalities in order to stay free," Raymond commented dryly. "Please, just come sit down and let me explain."

Roger glared and folded his arms, but Janet seemed intrigued.

"Alright then, I'll listen to what you have to say, and if at any moment I want to wash my hands of the whole mess, you'll agree to get up and leave without a fuss. Deal?" she asked, her gaze steady.

"Deal." Raymond blew out a sigh of relief.

CHAPTER SEVENTEEN

"This just don't seem right. I'm not liking this at all," Roger muttered, shaking his head, when he, Laney, Janet, and Raymond pulled into the driveway of Mayor Andrews' empty house the next evening.

"It's not a crime scene." Raymond shrugged. "And he left the house to me, so technically, we're all just going into my house."

They followed him to the front door, and he unlocked it, letting them all in.

"No one said we couldn't come here," he said, stepping into the foyer and closing the door behind himself.

"What are we even looking for?" Laney frowned.

"I'll know it when I see it," Janet replied. "Where's his bedroom?" she asked Raymond.

"Up the stairs and to the left."

Janet set off at a jog, taking the steps two at a time until she disappeared around the corner. Laney looked for guidance from Raymond, but he seemed to be lost in thought, gazing around the well-appointed home as if seeing it for the first time, so she decided to follow Janet. When Laney entered Mayor Andrews' bedroom, the silence of it feeling rather tomb-like, she found Janet sitting on the floor, searching through boxes that she had pulled out from under the bed. Not wanting to be a distraction, she stood in the corner, watching Janet, and when Roger and Raymond came up the stairs, she motioned for them to do the same.

They waited, each of them jumpy and on edge, for what seemed like an eternity while Janet sifted through at least five boxes of pictures and papers, until she reached the last one. When she opened the small stuffed-to-the-seams shoe box, its contents spilled out as if they were glad to be released.

"Didn't the police search this house after your father's death?" Janet asked Raymond, still digging through papers.

"Yeah, of course. They searched here and at his office." Raymond nodded, confused.

"Then why were these boxes untouched?" She raised an eyebrow at him.

"Because they were in the storage unit that he had. After he…" Raymond swallowed hard and cleared his throat. "After he…passed, I brought all of the things from his storage unit up here, so that I could sort through all of it at once. I think it's just old bills and stuff."

"And you didn't think to mention that to the police?" Janet blinked at him.

"I guess I just didn't see why some old papers would matter. The thought of telling the police never even occurred to me." Raymond shook his head, looking embarrassed.

Janet stared at him for a moment, lips pursed, then went back to her task. Laney had no idea what Janet was looking for, but when she saw Janet's facial expressions morph from determination, to curiosity, to understanding, she knew that the attorney had found something important.

Raymond also noticed the change in Janet's demeanor.

"What is it? What'd you find?" he asked, his voice brimming with cautious optimism. Janet thought for a moment, papers in hand, then focused on Raymond.

"I'm going to need more time to read through everything, but I think I may have just discovered a motive from the letters I skimmed."

"Letters?" Laney asked.

Janet nodded and gestured at the overflowing box.

"Child support agreement letters, and other paperwork that shows…" she broke off, glancing sympathetically at Raymond.

"That showed what?" Raymond demanded. "Just tell us what you found. My life and freedom could depend upon it."

Janet took a breath and released it slowly, dropping her gaze to the pile of letters and legal documents.

"I'm sorry, Raymond, but it seems that Mayor Andrews had another son."

Raymond went deathly pale and shook his head in disbelief, his eyes wide. "No. No way. That's impossible. How could my father have another son?"

His throat worked convulsively. "Are you saying that my dad had an affair? While my mom was sick all those years?" Raymond turned a pale shade of green and took a breath to steady himself.

Janet raised her hands, a signal that he needed to calm down.

"No, Raymond, there's more to it than that," she began carefully. "According to these letters, this was 36 years ago. How old are you?"

"Thirty-five. So...he had another family?" Raymond's debilitating rage turned to confusion and pain before their very eyes.

"I don't think that's true either." Janet shook her head. "Based on what I've read, your dad was in a relationship with someone when he was very young. When the young lady finally approached him with the news about the child, he was already the mayor of Iberden.

We'll have to dig into this more another time, but right now what's important is that the mayor's other son is right here in Iberden."

"But," Laney interrupted, unable to contain her curiosity. "How is it that no one in a tiny town like Iberden knows about this?"

Raymond spoke before Janet had the chance to answer. "He was hiding the other son, wasn't he? He was paying to keep all of this quiet..." He abruptly cut off his sentence, his jaw muscles flexing.

"I don't know for sure, but that's my hunch, particularly after reading some of the newer letters." Janet nodded.

"Raymond, at first, your dad wrote letters to the mother of the child, but once the child was of age, he wrote to the child instead, and has apparently maintained contact with him ever since," Janet explained.

The final piece of the puzzle suddenly fell into place for Laney and she gasped, amazed that she hadn't figured it out sooner.

"Matt," she exclaimed. "Matt is the mayor's other son. That's why he was so angry when I asked him to take me to your place in Brigton. He knew if we all got together, we'd figure out that none of us was the killer." She paused, taking in the solemn looks on the faces around her. She turned to Janet for confirmation. "I'm right, aren't I?" Laney asked.

Janet nodded, and Raymond turned beet red, looking as though he might blow a gasket. "I have a half-brother," he ground out, his voice hoarse. "And he killed my father because I had everything he wanted."

Janet gazed at him sympathetically. "And now we just need to prove it."

CHAPTER EIGHTEEN

Laney wracked her brain to remember all that she could of Matt's visit to the tea room. Trying to replay every last detail in her head, she landed on something that stuck in her craw. She knew, without a doubt, that she had locked the door before leaving that day, but it was open when she returned. Roger hadn't been home at the time and she'd been so distracted with getting her new purchases inside that she hadn't thought anything of it. But how could Matt have unlocked the door in the first place?

The window. Matt was easily tall enough to have climbed through the window in the parlor, but that still left one very important question - why was Mayor Andrews there? Laney couldn't wrap her head around that one. There had to be an explanation, it was just a matter of finding it.

"It doesn't really matter what the mayor was doing in the tea room," Janet insisted. "We can worry about that later - right now we need to find proof that Matt is the one who killed him."

Laney, Janet, Roger, and Raymond stood in the middle of the crime scene, having bypassed the tape that marked off the area, and carefully scoured the area for clues.

"We're not going to find anything." Raymond sighed. "The police have been through this area a million times - if they didn't find anything, how are we supposed to?"

Laney shook her head. Something inside told her they were overlooking something. *What are we missing?* Then a longshot popped into her mind.

"What about Babby, from the antique store? I was at her shop on the day of the murder, and she's the one who told me she would send Matt over to help with my things. I don't think anyone has even talked to her since this whole thing started. Maybe it's time to have a conversation with her."

Janet and Roger looked skeptical, and Raymond shook his head.

"What? Why?" Laney asked. She was already turning towards the door when Raymond replied.

"I can't go because I'm still a suspect, and if you barge into her shop with two other people, the only thing it'll probably do is make her clam up, even if she does know something," he pointed out.

"Good point." Laney nodded. "Well then it looks like I'll just have to go by myself."

It was 12 p.m. on a Monday. Babby's shop would be open, and Laney couldn't imagine that the elderly shopkeeper would be anywhere else.

——— ——

When Laney arrived at the antique store, a beaming Babby greeted her from behind the counter. The store was empty of patrons, so Laney was able to immediately begin her covert interrogation of the shopkeeper. Fortunately, Babby loved to chat, so it shouldn't be too terribly difficult to get her to open up.

"Hi, Babby." Laney grinned and leaned against the front counter.

"Hello, Miss Laney. It's good to see you," Babby replied seeming glad for the company. "How can I help you? You need more things for Marcy's Tea Room? Or has your project been put on hold because of everything that's happened?" The older woman sobered.

"Unfortunately, current events have definitely thrown my schedule off, but I'll still be working on opening up as soon as I can," Laney confided.

"Such a shame, that awful...event. I'm so looking forward to visiting the tea room again when you open. I miss that place." She smiled, remembering. "So, what can I do for you then, young lady?"

Laney took a breath and, sink or swim, decided to just dive right in. "Actually, I was hoping that you might be able to tell me a little bit about Matt."

"Matt the mail man?" Babby frowned, confused.

Laney nodded, deliberately maintaining a light-hearted expression.

"We're supposed to meet for dinner tonight, but I was hoping to know a little more about him before then." She smiled sweetly, crossing her fingers behind her back, and hoping that her tiny little fib wouldn't come back to bite her. She wasn't typically a person who believed that the ends justified the means, but desperate situations sometimes called for desperate measures.

"Well, how lovely! Matt has always been like a son to me." Babby clasped her hands together under her chin in delight. "I don't believe that he's ever dated a local girl before. Haven't seen him do much but work since his mom..." Her sentence trailed off and she sighed.

"What happened to his mom?" Laney asked, her pulse quickening. "He hasn't mentioned his parents to me yet. I didn't want to bring it up." She shrugged. That part, at least, was true. In the short conversations that she'd had with Matt, they'd never discussed his parents.

Babby shook her head sadly. "Not many people know, but Matt came to Iberden when he was maybe ten years old. Little string bean, he was. Came in one day out of the blue with his mom, but she was a bit of a loner, I must say. Didn't really talk to any of us."

"Odd that she'd settle into such a small town where she didn't know anyone," Laney commented, paying close attention. She didn't want to miss a single detail.

"She never did settle in exactly. At least not for long. Poor woman ended up getting killed in a car accident. She paid me to look after Matt, then went off on a weekend trip and never came back."

Laney noticed Babby's eyes grow moist. She blinked rapidly, then continued, "Matt must have been about sixteen then. His dad was never in the picture, so when his mama died, he had no other family. It was actually all a big to-do at the time. Mayor Andrews took it upon himself to get poor Matt situated and had him sent over to the orphanage in Brigton."

Laney's brows rose. "So, Matt came back here to Iberden when he was older?"

"Oh, yes. As soon as he turned 18, he was back here, looking for an apartment and applying for the open position at the post office. Been there ever since." Babby shrugged. "Not sure if I should have told you that much before your first date, but like I said, Matt is like a son to me. He's a good man, I can tell you that. Always helping me out over here at the shop to make extra cash - delivering furniture, balancing the books, locking up at night if he's the last one in the back room…"

Laney interrupted when a hunch hit her like a ton of bricks. "So, he helps run the store?"

"Unofficially." Babby nodded. "He's also known as quite the Mr. Fix-It here in town. A jack of all trades." She smiled proudly.

"I see," Laney fought to keep her voice casual, despite the importance of what she just heard. "Lots of hidden talents, eh?"

"I guess you could say that." Babby chuckled "Just the other week I got locked out of the store and Matt found some way to get me back inside before I could even call a locksmith."

Laney uttered a fake laugh, her mind suddenly flooded with a detailed memory. The bobby pin. After the mayor's body had been discovered, she'd found Roger sitting on the porch with a bobby pin in his hands, fidgeting, while lost in thought. Bingo. Laney had thought that perhaps both Matt and Mayor Andrews crawled inside the tea room through the parlor window, but what if Matt came in right through the front door? That would explain how he'd been able to get inside, commit the murder, or dump a body that was already dead, and be standing near his truck when she arrived. It all made sense, but there was one detail that Laney still had to chase down.

"Speaking of locks, I have a window at the tea room that needs one, and I'd like to get an antique if I can find one. You wouldn't happen to have anything like that around here, would you?" she asked innocently.

"You know, it's funny that you would ask." Babby cocked her head to the side. "I happen to have one that just showed up in the last week or so. It's pretty beat up, but you can take a look at it if you'd like. It's over by the display of hand tools." She pointed to a quaint display made with rough-hewn crates, a hay bale, and a couple of bushel baskets.

"Oh, great, thanks – I'll definitely take a look."

Laney tried to look nonchalant as she made her way to the display, and her heart nearly exploded within her chest when she saw a window lock that exactly matched all the others in the tea room. It was broken.

Taking a tissue out of her pocket, so that she didn't disturb any potential evidence, Laney gingerly picked up the lock from the underside and took it to Babby at the counter.

"I found it, and I'd like to take it, if you don't mind." She smiled, hoping that the elderly woman wouldn't hear her thudding heart. "What do I owe you?"

"Oh, honey, I'm not going to charge you for that beat up old thing." Babby waved a hand. "If you can make use of it, just take it. It'd only sit here and gather dust otherwise."

"Thank you so much." Laney smiled, feeling a bit faint. "Do you have a little bag?"

Before she knew it, Laney was striding quickly down Maple Path, with her piece of evidence tucked neatly into a small plastic bag.

CHAPTER NINETEEN

One Month Later

Laney heard the bells over the front door of Marcy's Tea Room jangle and looked up to see a trio of people in the foyer. There was a young couple that she didn't recognize and behind them was Babby, strolling in on her afternoon break.

"Wow, Laney! You really outdid yourself in here!" Babby's eyes widened with obvious delight as she took in the newly painted walls, upcycled furnishings, and wonderfully mismatched place settings. "It looks much more cozy and comfy than it did before." She beamed.

"Thanks, Babby." Laney blushed at the compliment. "But honestly, I couldn't have done any of this without you." She had to give credit where credit was due.

After Laney delivered the lock and told Detective Worth about the bobby pin, with Roger backing her up, Babby had agreed to come down to the station with her to make a statement. When Worth had remained a bit skeptical, the feisty old woman had squared her shoulders, looked the detective straight in the eye and told her what was what. Then she broke down crying because she had just implicated a man who had been like a son to her in a horrific crime. But it had been the right thing to do. When it came right down to it, poor Babby had felt like she had no choice. Even though Matt would have to pay the consequences, she had to tell the truth. Her truth, plus that of the others made it much easier for Detective Worth to trace the series of events back to Matt.

Once Worth had all the information, she went to the judge for a search warrant and had Officer Bonham take Matt to a holding cell while she and the forensics team did their jobs. Stashed in Matt's garage they found the murder weapon and a stack of letters from Mayor Andrews. When they explored the backyard, they found the site of the murder in Matt's shed. There was DNA evidence on the floor of the insulated shop that was conclusive. That explained why none of Laney's neighbors had heard a gunshot. The Mayor was obviously killed in the nearly soundproof shed, transported to the tea room in the mail truck, where more DNA was eventually found, and tossed into the parlor through the broken window. Bloodied tarps, that had been used to transport the body, were stashed in rafters in Matt's garage.

Laney led Babby to a table by the windows, that was set with delicate pink china, and the older woman squeezed her hand in gratitude. Not for the first time since opening the tea room, Laney was reminded of her beloved grandmother, and finally, now that she was living and working in Grandma Marcy's home, her thoughts of the dear woman made her smile. Moving forward in her life and fulfilling her grandmother's wish had made her grief and loneliness easier to bear, and now she was able to smile and laugh with abandon, knowing somehow that Marcy would be so tickled to see the tea room booming again.

There were meaningful touches everywhere that reminded Laney of Grandma Marcy – the frilly apron hanging behind the register, the leather guest book, the heavenly scent of freshly baked bread, pastries, and other goodies that she'd learned to bake by standing on a stool next to her grandmother in this very kitchen.

Laney was also able to use her own skills in art to help make the tea room a destination for tourists and locals alike once more. She'd hand-painted every chair, she made all of the graphics and promotional materials for the busy tea room, and she'd even made a teacup shaped sign that she painted herself. It had become the new Marcy's Tea Room logo when she created her website, and she was considering renting out some of the other rooms in the huge Victorian home as temporary guest lodging.

Her days were filled with tasks, most of which she loved, and within weeks, Laney had been able to hire a small staff for the cooking, serving, and cleaning, so that she could focus on making sure that Marcy's Tea Room was the coziest place in town, with the best food and atmosphere.

She had her memories. She had new friends and family. And finally, after searching for years to find her niche, Laney had a home that she loved. As she glanced around the busy dining room, filled with both familiar and new faces, she was filled with gratitude for what she had, and excited to see what might be in her future. It was exhilarating to realize that her adventures at Marcy's Tea Room had just begun, and she couldn't wait to find out what else life had in store for all of them – Laney, Roger, Janet, and even Raymond, who had just come in the front door, favoring her with a smile the size of Texas.

Giving Raymond a little wave, Laney went over to check on Babby.

"How's your tea?" she asked, delighted to see that the older woman had taken a sip, closed her eyes and smiled.

"Oh, honey, I've been waiting for this since your grandma closed down," Babby raised her cup in tribute. "Best tea in Iberden!"

AUTHOR'S NOTE

I'd love to hear your thoughts on my books, the story-lines, and anything else that you'd like to comment on —reader feedback is very important to me. My contact information, along with some other helpful links, is listed on the next page. If you'd like to be on my list of "folks to contact" with updates, release and sales notifications, etc.... just shoot me an email and let me know. Thanks for reading!

Also...

... if you're looking for more great reads, Summer Prescott Books publishes several popular series by outstanding Cozy Mystery authors.

CONTACT SUMMER PRESCOTT
BOOKS PUBLISHING

Twitter: @summerprescott1

Bookbub: https://www.bookbub.com/authors/summer-prescott

Blog and Book Catalog: http://summerprescottbooks.com

Email: summer.prescott.cozies@gmail.com

YouTube: https://www.youtube.com/channel/UCngKNUkDdWuQ5k7-Vkfrp6A

And…be sure to check out the Summer Prescott Cozy Mysteries fan page and Summer Prescott Books Publishing Page on Facebook – let's be friends!

To download a free book, and sign up for our fun and exciting newsletter, which will give you opportunities to win prizes and swag, enter contests, and be the first to know about New Releases, click here: http://summerprescottbooks.com

Made in United States
North Haven, CT
09 March 2022

16939035R00095